Watercolor
WHISPERS

GLORIA BOSTIC

Year of the Book
135 Glen Avenue
Glen Rock, PA 17327

Print ISBN: 978-1-64649-086-8
eBook ISBN: 978-1-64649-087-5

Library of Congress Control Number: 2020909415

DEDICATION

To Lee, for always supporting me.

Acknowledgments

To you, COVID-19,

you came into our lives, changed our plans, filled us with dread,

and robbed us of so many things in the year 2020.

We lost trips and time with people we love,

Lost freedom to move about our world—

You even took away people we love,

But you couldn't steal our spirit.

We found ways to keep going.

We cleaned and did crafts.

We cooked and baked.

We sang and danced.

We used ZOOM.

We met online.

And we wrote books!

℘ROLOGUE

℘ummeled by icy daggers, every cell in Detective Ron Bishop's body screamed to wake up from his fifteen-year-old nightmare. Freezing shower shards cut through the 5:00 A.M. drowsiness. He knew he needed to be awake—wide awake and in the present—when he reached the crime scene.

Ron never got used to these calls. It didn't matter if they came in the light of day or, like this one, waking him from a dead sleep. The result was the same.

His days as a detective had taught him that answering a call like this one required more than being fully awake. He needed to be razor-sharp by the time he got to the park. He needed to do his job well so *this* murder would not go unpunished. *This murderer* would pay.

The calendar might say early spring, but the chill of the morning mist belied its tale. Arriving on the scene a mere forty minutes later, Bishop pushed his way through the brush, shoved his hands deep in his jacket pockets and waited for the young officer who approached shaking his head in disbelief.

"What have we got?" The detective pulled out his pen and notepad.

"No ID. Nothing but her body, thrown in the ditch like so much garbage, covered with dirt—not much of a grave." The officer shook his head again. "I guess when the bastard finished beating her to death, he was suddenly in a hurry." Looking back over his shoulder he added, "Wouldn't have taken much longer to drag her down to the lake."

Bishop recognized the revulsion on the younger man's face and knew it wasn't going to be pretty. He was right. Upon closer examination he understood why. At first glance all he could tell

1

was she had blonde hair. But with a closer look, he saw how attractive she must have been. The side of her face that wasn't swollen and bloody was striking. But now, covered in mud and blood, the left side of her face was shattered. Another Jane Doe. But he hated calling her that. She was somebody's daughter... could be somebody's wife, mother... or *sister*.

Who are you, lady? And who in the hell did this to you?

CHAPTER ONE

When the invisible hand guided hers, Mia Reed knew the image would hold a message—a crucial message—possibly a matter of life or death. But on this Tuesday morning her hand was her own as she looked at her newest client's intake information. Frederick Allen Alessi, Jr. had fallen down the steps of his home and suffered a broken tibia and depressed skull fracture. Neurosurgery was successful. The symptom most relevant for her art therapy would be his resulting memory loss. Mia thought this would be a new challenge, but she had no idea how one patient would turn her world upside-down.

Before heading to Mr. Alessi's room to get a more complete history, Mia checked her appearance. She'd been so anxious to have a look at her new patient's file that she had dropped her backpack on the desk and tossed her jacket on the hook when she arrived. It wasn't until now she saw how the wind had wrecked her hair, and the mirror reflected nothing resembling a professional. *I am a hot mess!*

Although she was becoming more comfortable in her new role, there were still insecurities. She was a mere intern, and imagined or not, knew she was being judged all the time. Her step-sister Julie, though only months her senior, had the look of a sophisticated woman, while Mia appeared years younger. But then Julie had always matured more quickly—physically—than Mia. She had been the first to need a training bra, to get her period, to wear makeup, and to have a boyfriend. But none of that had ever bothered Mia. She was her own person with her own very specific vision of what she wanted to do with her life. That had become as clear as a calling many years ago.

Yet Mia now struggled, seeing her youthful look as an obstacle to accomplishing her goals. Could she really help people if they didn't take her seriously? At times she wondered if she would get the chance to use her special gift at all.

At twenty-three, Mia had accomplished more than many her age—even her sister—but looking like an eighteen-year-old often made it difficult for others to believe in her. She remembered her first session with one of her older patients, Mrs. Perry, who asked what high school she would be graduating from. She remembered how her cheeks had burned with embarrassment as she explained she'd be graduating from Seton Hill University.

Having restored her hair to its more manageable bob, Mia hurried back to her office space and wondered if she would get a similar reaction from this Mr. Alessi whose chart she'd reviewed. *Frederick A. Alessi, looks like you've been through a lot.*

She had no idea just how right she was. A quick check of the time reminded her she was due in the young man's room in the south wing to introduce herself and complete a more detailed intake than the initial one provided.

Since she'd become quite familiar with the hospital's layout, it didn't take long for Mia to reach his room and not much longer to determine Alessi was suffering from depression as well as the injuries he'd sustained in the accident. Though he glanced in her direction when she walked in, his gaze immediately returned to some spot in the distance.

The other gentleman in the room leapt to his feet and introduced himself as Frederick's brother, and she noticed the patient's flat affect was in sharp contrast to his sibling's animated countenance. Anthony Alessi, she would learn, was the older brother. It didn't take long for Mia to see how protective he was of Frederick—and as she would later learn, had always been—but at this moment she simply wished he would stop answering for his brother and let him speak for himself.

"Mr. Alessi," she said at last, "why don't you go get yourself a coffee and relax for a bit? I'll come get you when we're through here."

"No, I'm fine really. I'll just hang out over here if you don't mind," he said heading for the chair in the corner.

"I do mind," Mia answered a little too curtly. The way her patient's eyes opened wider, he must have caught the edge in her voice. She hadn't meant for it to come out so harshly, but the last thing she needed was a family member judging her as she conducted her interview. "I'm sorry, sir. It's just that we find our patients usually answer our questions more freely without a third party in the room." Mia hoped this interloper would accept her professional opinion and remove himself, but she discovered he wasn't so easily persuaded.

"Oh, don't worry Miss—Reed is it? Freddie knows he can speak freely in front of me... right, Freddie? You don't want me to leave, do you?"

Little brother finally spoke. "Anthony, go get a coffee... please." Looking up from his bed ever so briefly, he exchanged a look with his brother... a peculiar look Mia couldn't quite read.

Anthony headed for the door with a quick glance back. "I won't be long," he said.

"There's no need to hurry, really." Mia threw him her most genuine, charming smile in an effort to erase her earlier irritability.

"The name's Anthony, and like I said, I won't be long." Then he did something unexpected and truly baffling. He smiled at his younger brother, after which a slower, slyer smile curled his lips as he looked at Mia and gave her a wink.

Even more surprising to Mia was the warm flush that instantly filled her cheeks.

"So, Frederick," she said. "Looks like you've been through a lot."

"Yeah, I guess you could say that," he said resting back on his pillows. "And I don't go by Frederick... or Fred, before you ask. That's my father. I'm Freddie."

CHAPTER TWO

"Are you okay, little brother?"

"Whaddya think, Anthony?" Freddie asked. "I'm in this bed with a fractured skull, one leg that hurts like hell, and I can't remember shit. Claire hasn't even come in to see me," he said with a mix of frustration and despair.

Anthony hurried to reassure him. "Don't worry, Claire texted me and said she'll be here as soon as she gets off work."

"Why the hell did she text you instead of me?"

Anthony dropped in the chair by the bed and put his hand on his brother's shoulder. "Shh, calm down, buddy. She was probably worried you might be resting and didn't want to wake you. What's got you so worked up, anyhow?" He pulled his chair closer still and leaned in. "Was it that therapist... Ms. Reed? Was she asking a lot of questions? What did you tell her?"

Freddie covered his face with both hands, and pulled them back to run through his hair—his habit when upset—but dropped them quickly onto his lap when he touched the bandage. It only served to renew the throbbing pain.

"She was all right. Just getting history... and I told her the same thing I've been telling everybody else. I don't remember!" he shouted shattering the quiet hospital atmosphere.

The day-nurse, who'd been tending to a patient in the next room, heard his shouting and rushed in to see what was wrong. Before she could even ask, Anthony assured her everything was okay. "Thanks for checking, Morgan, but we're good. Freddie was just letting out some frustration. Right, bud?" he said turning back to his brother.

Freddie nodded as his expression morphed from angry to vacant.

7

Alone again, he saw Anthony studying his face before asking, "So, do you remember anything yet?"

"No, nothing," Freddie muttered. The creases in his forehead deepened with the effort.

"C'mon, don't let it get to you, bud. I mean, you fell down the steps. Does it really matter why? The important thing is I found you, and you're going to be all right."

Freddie saw the concern in Anthony's eyes. "Yeah, you know, they said if you hadn't shown up when you did, it could have been much worse. I can't believe how lucky I am that you came around that afternoon. It's kinda weird..."

"No, not weird, just fortunate. Like I told you," Anthony interrupted, "I was on my way to the club to sneak in nine holes, and driving down your road, I saw that unfamiliar car come out of your driveway. I knew you and Claire weren't usually home at that hour." Anthony shrugged. "Something told me to pull into your lane and make sure everything was okay. Then when I saw your car, I figured I'd stop in and say a quick hello." Shaking his head, he added, "The broken glass and front door ajar sent me flying in to find you laying there at the bottom of the steps. I gotta tell ya, you about scared me to death, bud."

"If only I could remember. Like, why the hell was I home at one o'clock in the afternoon? And, I mean, how can I help the police find the sonofabitch who did this to me if I can't remember anything?"

The frustration and effort shot new pain through his head and his hands flew to his face again in an attempt to quell it.

Anthony rushed to calm him. "Look, I don't think you should push yourself to remember like this. It's making your headache worse."

Freddie groaned and dropped his head back into the pillow. "You just don't get it. You don't know what it's like to be stuck in this bed—alone—not knowing why..."

"Hey, you're not alone. I'm here for you, kid, and I'm not going anywhere."

"Yeah, yeah, I know—and I appreciate it, really—but, but Claire... Jeeze, she's my wife. Why isn't she here?" Freddie squeezed his eyes shut and hung his head. "I just don't get it. I mean, she couldn't take time off from work with me lying here like this?"

"C'mon, little brother. You know what it's like for teachers. Maybe they couldn't get a substitute for her or something."

Freddie knew his big brother wanted to make him feel better, but it wasn't working. He couldn't tell Anthony how strained his relationship with his wife had become lately. Big brother was a bachelor enjoying his carefree lifestyle—a lifestyle their parents' money had provided—and seemed to think Freddie's marriage was perfect. Perfect for him, that is.

Freddie knew his brother had no intentions of settling down himself. And he hadn't missed the smile and wink he'd shot at the kid therapist either.

"So let's talk about something else and get your mind off all this," Anthony said.

"All right, let's talk about you putting the moves on my new therapist." Freddie knew how susceptible most women were to his brother's charm, and he often wondered why Anthony got the dark good looks of a Hugh Jackman while he was left with mousey brown hair and a plain countenance.

"What? Don't be ridiculous. She's a child."

"*Hmph*, that's never stopped you before, and she's not a child, really. Too young for you though."

"What's that supposed to mean?" Anthony asked, a look of innocence somewhat masking the amusement Freddie saw in his eyes.

"I asked since she looked so young, but she said she's twenty-three. That's almost ten years younger than you." The effort it took to look up at his brother who was still standing by his bedside aggravated his headache, and he pushed the call button.

"What's wrong? What do you need?" Anthony asked.

But that quickly his nurse appeared at the door. At Freddie's request she checked his chart, agreed it had been long enough, and went to get his pain meds. By the time she returned, Anthony had agreed to leave and let his little brother get some rest. They both knew the meds would allow him to sleep. Freddie took his pills, sank back onto his pillows, and watched his brother follow Morgan from the room. He couldn't help wondering if she would be Anthony's next conquest.

Whatever, he thought. *I've got the only woman I'll ever need.* But his final thought as the meds eased him into sleep was, *Or do I?*

CHAPTER THREE

$\mathcal{M}$ia shrugged into her jacket, threw her backpack on her shoulder, and headed down the hall. It had been a long day—not in hours but in stress—and she was anxious to put this one behind her.

"See you at home," Mia mouthed to her roommate as she passed the nurse's station.

Morgan raised a finger, signaling she had something to tell her but needed a moment. Mia hoped her roommate's phone call would quickly end. Closing her eyes for a moment, she sighed. Her wish was granted; Morgan put the phone down mere seconds later. "What's up?"

"Nothing major, but I thought you'd want to know Alessi in room #215 has become increasingly agitated this afternoon. It started after you left and that good-looking brother of his came back." Morgan placed her hand on her heart and looked heavenward when she mentioned Anthony. This made Mia smile since she saw him more as an arrogant intruder than anyone to swoon over. "He slept for a while after his meds, but when he woke, he was even more worked up."

"You don't think it was anything I did, do you?" Mia asked. After all they hadn't even begun any therapy. It couldn't have been just from taking his history, she hoped. But then she had pressed him a little to see how much he could remember from the day he was hurt. "Do you think I should check on him before I go?" Still plagued by insecurities, Mia looked for guidance but wasn't thrilled when Morgan said it might be a good idea. That soothing cup of herbal tea would have to wait a little longer.

When Mia got to room #215, she quickly found her roommate's concerns to be justified. Instead of the passive, docile patient she'd spent time with earlier in the day, she found an animated, fretful man whose visage barely resembled what she'd observed during her interview.

Freddie's head snapped up when she came through the door, and Mia observed an expression—was it hope?—that quickly vanished upon his recognition of her. *Well that's not very encouraging.* "What do you want?" he asked irritably.

"I... I just thought I'd check in on you before I left for the day. I'm sorry if I disturbed you." Mia lowered her head and turned to leave. *Maybe this wasn't such a good idea.*

"Wait... I'm sorry. No really, Mia... it is Mia, right?" At her nod, he continued. "I thought, I mean I was hoping Claire was finally here."

"Your wife hasn't been in yet? I'm sorry, Freddie. I'm sure she'll be here soon." Mia was torn. Though the couch in her apartment beckoned, she wondered if there wasn't more she could do to help him. He looked so forlorn. "Would you like me to stay a while, or is there anything I can get you?"

"No," he said with an edge in his voice. "Not unless you can get me my wife." The words *my wife* dripped with bitterness.

"Well, I'm heading out, but I can check at the desk and see if they've heard anything." After a pause with no response, she added, "I'm sure she'll be here soon, Freddie."

"Whatever," was his only response as he rolled his face toward the window. Mia's dislike for Claire Alessi was growing. What kind of a wife was she anyway?

Finding Morgan in the hall, she filled her in and explained she was pretty sure the only medicine that could help Freddie Alessi right now was for his wife to show up. "Has she called?"

"No, and I did try to get in touch with her, but it went straight to voicemail. I can't say I was overly tactful in the message I left." Morgan shook her head. "I hope she's got a good reason for not getting in here. Unbelievable."

"Yeah, I'm trying not to judge, but it's hard."

Mia's strong Christian upbringing had given her faith that most people did their best and taught her to believe everyone was a child of God. But that didn't mean she was blind to the evil in the world. And she knew there were people who, for whatever reason, had a darker walk… like the man who had kidnapped and held her prisoner when she was a mere adolescent. That man's dark past had left him twisted and, though she forgave him, she secretly hoped he'd never get out of the mental facility where he now resided.

Shaking off the ugly memory as well as her ill-feelings toward Claire Alessi, Mia pulled her jacket tightly around her and rushed to her car at last. She hoped this final chilly spell would be the last cold snap now that spring had arrived, and caught herself grinning as she drove past a row of forsythia bushes with bright yellow blossoms of hope. The scenery here in the Pittsburgh area was different from back home, but these blooms reminded her of the ones bordering her family property, and with the memory returned the familiar nostalgia and homesickness.

Unlike her roommate, she had a wonderful family, and the decision to move away had been difficult. Doing her postgraduate work at Seton Hill had been a no-brainer, but she still wondered if the decision to stay and work there was the right one.

Arriving back at the apartment, she dismissed her doubts, and while her tea was steeping, put her shoes in the closet, trading them for the comfy cushiness of slippers, and slid her bra from under her sweater. "Ah," she breathed with the relief every woman knows.

Carrying her tea to the living area she shared with Morgan, Mia curled up in the "big brown beast," as they'd nicknamed the oversized, overstuffed chair by the window, and sorted the mail. It wasn't long before Simeon curled up on her lap. Warmed by the affection of the Persian, she absently stroked his beautiful fur.

Most of the mail was tossed aside when she recognized her sister's handwriting on one envelope and quickly ripped it open. "Oh, Simmie, this one's from Julie," she said to her rather disinterested cat.

Her sister was ridiculously busy meeting article deadlines and working on her first attempt at a full-length novel, yet she always found time to write to Mia at least once a week. Instead of diminishing her homesickness, all the latest on their brothers, Cody and Bobby, and little sister, Destiny, and their parents added to her longing for home and family. After reading the final *"See you soon, little sister. Love you,"* Mia put the letter aside and reached for her laptop, nudging Simeon to the side.

"Don't look at me like that," Mia said. "You know the drill." His stare asked for more. "Yes, I'll brush you after dinner. Now scoot."

But before the cat had even become situated or the laptop started up, Morgan burst through the door.

With a quick "Hey," she headed straight for the kitchen to grab a diet soda and bag of chips. "What do you feel like for dinner?" she asked falling onto the couch with her pre-dinner snack. Morgan James had a continuous battle with her weight that left her always thinking about the next meal. "Wanna call Grubhub and get something delivered? I'm beat."

"Sure, but not pizza again, okay?"

"All right. Chinese maybe?" Morgan said opening the drawer in the side table where she kept all the take-out menus. "I could go for the beef lo mein, and I'll call it in. What do you want?"

Mia's thoughts were on her family more than her stomach. "Order me some wonton soup and a couple of spring rolls," she said, then turned her attention to sending Julie a quick email thanking her for the newsy letter. Though she admired her sister's habit of sending handwritten letters and cards, she found it much easier and less time consuming to correspond electronically. She was thinking about face-timing Julie later when her thoughts were interrupted.

"By the way," Morgan said, "that guy's wife still hadn't shown up when I left. I was gonna call her cell again, but that good-looking brother showed up and said he'd take care of it. What's his name again?"

"The brother? Anthony. I remember because he looked like an Anthony... not a Tony." Seeing the puzzled look on her roommate's face, she laughed and added, "I knew a Tony in high school and he was such a cool, likable guy. This Anthony character strikes me as being full of himself."

"Really? Boy, he must have really rubbed you the wrong way," Morgan said. "Regardless, I know he's been there for his brother. He seems like a pretty good guy to me."

Mia knew her roommate was right. The way Anthony Alessi cared about his younger brother and wanted to protect him, maybe he wasn't all bad... and he was definitely good-looking. But still...

CHAPTER FOUR

Freddie wiped his forehead with the back of his hand. "I told you I can't remember." The wooden words articulated his weariness with the detective's interrogation. He knew the guy was just doing his job, but Freddie was exhausted, and his head ached with the effort to recall the events that left him in his current situation.

"I'm sorry, Mr. Alessi, but anything you recall from that day, any little details at all, might help us find whoever is responsible." Ronald Bishop looked at the few notes and observations he'd jotted in his scratchpad, then looked back at Freddie. "What is the last thing you do remember, sir?"

The crease between Freddie's eyes deepened in his effort to recollect anything from that morning. He finally answered, "I remember going to work. I remember getting to the office," he said slowly turning his wedding band round and round.

"So you don't remember going home." Bishop said it as more of a statement than a question and only glanced fleetingly to see the patient shaking his head. After a long pause Freddie raised his eyes to Bishop then turned them toward his brother.

"That's enough," Anthony said. "Look, my brother's exhausted, and besides, he's told you everything he remembers." He got up from the chair where he'd been sitting quietly throughout the brief interview and put his hand on his little brother's shoulder.

Freddie gratefully sank back into his pillows, allowing big brother to handle the detective who simply nodded.

"Okay," Bishop said, laying his card on the tray by the patient's bed. "But if you think of anything, anything at all, let me know." The detective turned back as he reached the door. "Say, I've tried to reach Mrs. Alessi with no luck. Would you have her get in touch with me, please? Just a few questions..."

"Anthony, what the hell's going on? Where is she?" Freddie looked to his brother for answers. For help. He couldn't stop the endless swirl of questions spinning round and round in his aching head. He needed someone to help him. And he had always looked to Anthony when he needed help before. When Freddie was only five and his brother Tony was ten, big brother was the one who'd helped him learn to ride his bike. And when Tony had discovered his attraction to the opposite sex and abruptly insisted on being called Anthony as a sixteen-year-old, he still looked out for his little brother, eventually introducing him to the girl who would become his wife.

His wife... why hadn't Claire called or been in to see him? He remembered opening his eyes in the ER and searching for her. But all he saw was his brother and the fear in his brother's eyes. Anthony said he knew Claire was worried sick, yet if she was so worried about him, why hadn't he seen or heard from her since he got to the hospital Monday night?

"I don't know what to tell you, buddy," Anthony said looking from Freddie to the detective and back. "But I'm sure she'll probably be in after school lets out this afternoon."

"Your wife's a teacher?" Bishop asked looking at Freddie.

"Yeah, but they could've gotten a substitute for her."

"Where does she teach?" Jotting down the name of the school and glancing at his notes he added, "Maybe I can catch up with her there."

"Well, if you do, you might let her know her husband would appreciate a visit," Freddie muttered.

"Sure thing." Ron Bishop, appearing to suddenly be in a hurry, turned to leave and ran smack into the young woman rushing in the door.

***

"Whoa, sorry... Mrs. Alessi?"

"Hardly," Mia said regaining her balance and pulling from the arms that had caught her and kept her upright. She had no idea who this handsome stranger might be, but she didn't appreciate nearly being knocked down.

"This is the lovely Miss Reed, Freddie's art therapist." Anthony had jumped to his feet and rushed to her side as though to rescue her.

Standing between the two men and looking up from one to the other, she was struck by the difference in their attractiveness. Anthony had the dark alluring look of an Italian Romeo, while this new stranger immediately made her remember her Grandma Val's heartthrob, a young Paul Newman... or maybe Chris Pine, an actor of her generation with those same mesmerizing blue eyes. *And they can both get out of my way.* Mia pushed past them and placed her attention where it needed to be.

"Good morning, Freddie." It still felt strange to call a twenty-seven-year-old man Freddie, but when she'd called him Frederick, which was the name on the chart, he'd quickly corrected her. "If your visitors don't mind, we can get started," she said with her brightest smile. The smile faded as she turned toward the two gentlemen at the door. "Would you mind?"

"Not at all. I was just leaving," Bishop said making a hasty exit.

"Do I have a choice?" Anthony asked.

Mia ignored the snide look. "Not really," she said as pleasantly as she could, but the expression on big brother's face said he wasn't happy about it.

Finally, alone with her patient, Mia wondered how receptive he might be, considering his agitated state. She took the time to reassure him there was no pressure to remember or to create an art piece to be judged. "Let's just get started and see where it takes us, okay?" Freddie nodded his begrudging assent and accepted the supplies he'd need. Since he'd chosen just drawing, she gave him a sketchpad and watched as he stared at the blank page.

She understood his hesitation and reminded him there was no urgency. "Just take your time, Freddie. No pressure," she said. "Remember, our treatment plan... and the theme you chose?"

"Yes, we decided I'd stop trying to remember for now and use it to relax."

"That's right. Good." Mia sat back in the chair she'd taken by the head of the bed and tried to mirror the relaxation she wished for him. She was relieved when the pencil finally began to move. His pencil strokes were hesitant at first but gradually flowed more easily. It helped that he didn't fret about his own lack of talent. So many of her patients struggled with this, saying, *"But I can't draw."* And she noticed Freddie actually did have some ability as the images took form on the page.

When it was done and he looked at his work, Freddie's brow knitted, he dropped his pencil, and fell back into the pillows propped behind him.

Mia hadn't asked any questions as he'd worked on his art but observed the smoothing of facial tension. Now he seemed almost as stressed as before he began.

"This is quite interesting, Freddie. Can you tell me about the home you've drawn?"

"It's my house."

"I like all the detail." She noticed the garage door was opened. Usually when someone drew a house with a garage, the door was down. "Is that a car in the garage?"

"Yeah." The crease between his brows deepened.

"Is that your car parked inside?"

"No. Mine is silver, not blue," he answered. Yet this was a pencil drawing with no color. Mia wondered why he saw it as a blue car.

She studied the drawing again noting the added pressure he'd used to shade the car. *But it could be silver.* "Hmm, this is interesting, Freddie. It's dark in the garage. Maybe the shadows are deceiving and it's actually silver, huh?"

"No," he said vehemently. "It's navy blue!"

"Okay, yes, I think I can see that now." The goal of this session had been to help her patient relax. To argue the point could further agitate him. But it was certainly curious.

CHAPTER FIVE

Back in her office, Mia finished her notes then picked up Freddie's pencil drawing and felt it pulling her in. Her fingers itched in a familiar way. Glancing at her book to be sure she hadn't forgotten anything, she saw her time was now her own.

Mia grabbed everything she needed, moved to her easel and allowed the watercolors to whisper their message through her fingers. She no longer thought about what she would put on the canvas but simply allowed the brush to take over.

The minutes passed with Mia completely lost in her work until a knock on her opened door pulled her away.

"You still here, Mia?" Morgan checked her watch. "I thought you'd be curled up in the beast by now."

"And that's exactly where I'm heading," Mia said noting the time.

"Got caught up in one of your painting trances, did ya?"

"Yeah, I guess I did, but now I'm outta here." Without a glance at the work on the easel, she stood, stretched, and added, "I'm just gonna clean up here and head out, but if you're leaving now, do you want to stop and get us some dinner? After the day I've had, I don't feel like cooking."

"Cool, how about Primanti Brothers?" Morgan couldn't get enough of the Pitts-Burgher Cheese Steak. "What do you want?"

"Definitely not what you're having." Mia shot her friend a big grin. "Just get me some vegetable soup and their chef salad."

With her supplies cleaned and everything carefully reorganized, Mia grabbed her jacket, but before leaving glimpsed a detail in her watercolor that had eluded her until this second. She moved closer and squinted at the car she'd painted in the open garage. *Well, I'll be... It is blue!*

Completely lost in thought as she pulled her office door closed, Mia turned and found herself face to face with Anthony Alessi. Startled, she stepped back and looked up into his curious brown eyes. Realizing he was studying her, she felt the heat rise in her cheeks. *Why doesn't he get out of the way?*

"I'm glad I caught you, Mia. Sorry, may I call you Mia? That's how Freddie refers to you when he talks about your sessions."

"That's fine. Now, if you'll excuse me, I've had a long day."

"Of course..." but he didn't step out of the way. "I wondered if you might have time for a quick coffee."

The suggestion caught Mia off-guard, and she stammered her reply. "I don't drink coffee."

"Oh, well... would you prefer something a little stronger?"

"No," she spat indignantly.

"I'm sorry, Mia. I didn't mean to insult you. I just thought maybe we could share a beverage and discuss Freddie's progress. I'm truly concerned about him."

Mia felt a bit ashamed of her brash response and tried to change her tone. "I'm sorry. I didn't mean to be abrupt. It's just that I've had a long day and was finally heading home." The way Anthony's eyes voiced his disappointment touched her, and before she could change her mind, she added, "Well, I do drink tea."

Anthony's face lit with what looked to her like a mix of relief and pleasure which, she had to admit, somehow gratified her.

But it wasn't until later, staring into her teacup, that Mia became aware of a niggling question slipping into her consciousness. *What does he really want from me?* As though reading her mind, Anthony answered her unspoken concern.

"Mia, I appreciate all you're trying to do for my little brother— I mean that—and I am comforted by your reassurances for an optimistic outcome." Mia thought that concluded their conversation and put her hands on the table preparing to leave, but he wasn't done. He put one of his hands over hers, quickly drawing it back when she gasped and stiffened. "I'm sorry... but I, I had another reason for wanting to talk with you."

"I think I've told you all I can about your brother's progress. We've only just begun to work together."

"Yes, I know. I mean that's not what I wanted to talk about." With his most charming smile he added, "I like you."

"What? Well thanks, I appreciate the vote of confidence." Mia felt another flush rising from her neck.

"No, I mean yes, I'm sure you must be good at what you do. But that's not what I'm talking about." Anthony chuckled. "This is me very awkwardly telling you I'd like to see you again but not as my little brother's therapist. I was thinking perhaps we could have lunch tomorrow—or dinner?"

Mia felt her phone vibrate and hurriedly checked it without responding. "Oh, sorry, Mr. Alessi..."

"Anthony, please."

"Right, well sorry, Anthony, but that was Morgan—my roommate—wondering where I am. I really should go." Mia grabbed her things and dashed away without another word, leaving Anthony, who had jumped to his feet, standing alone with his jaw on the floor.

Thanks for saving me, Morgan. Mia wasn't sure why she felt alarmed, and she knew her hasty retreat was rude, but Mia needed time to process what had just happened—and how she felt about it.

She replayed the conversation in her mind the whole way home. Finally accepting that he was asking her out—that he liked her that way—had her mind spinning madly. After all, he was her client's brother. Would going out with him even be ethical? *But then, he's not my patient.*

CHAPTER SIX

After ringing the bell twice, Detective Bishop banged on the door, but Freddie Alessi's wife didn't answer. He tried the phone number he'd been given for her cell and it still went straight to voicemail. It just didn't add up.

The Alessi brothers had both assured him Claire Alessi loved her husband, so why hadn't she visited? *Unless...*

Ron Bishop's visit to the school where she taught hadn't helped either. With school closed Easter Monday, the day of the break-in and assault on Alessi, and the text they'd received that she had the flu, school administrators had lined up a sub for the rest of the week and thought no more of it.

Bishop needed answers. He got back in the car, checked his notes and called the number he'd jotted down for Alessi's brother.

"Yeah, Mr. Alessi, I need your help. Okay, Anthony it is. So listen, I'm at your brother's house... yeah, at the front door, but the wife isn't answering." Bishop waited rolling his eyes. "I know the school said she's sick, but I've got to talk to her. I know it's getting late, but I need you to come over here with a key so we can check on her anyway, make sure she's okay."

Ending the call, he stared at the house—the house that might hold answers to many of his questions. It looked innocent enough. Nice enough. Certainly a lot better than his place in the city. *But he knew that didn't mean anything.*

This time the crime didn't have such dire consequences—just one guy with non-life-threatening injuries—could've been a lot worse. And Bishop knew how much worse a break-in could turn out. People should be safe in their own homes. But he knew they weren't.

He'd never forget that night when he was only fifteen, and lost in the music blasting through his headphones. And he could never forget the horrific scene he'd discovered when the music ended. His love for Metallica ended as well. "I Disappear" by his once favorite group became his nightmare's theme. That's when he learned no one was safe. And that's when the seeds of hatred were planted and began to fester. Now his life was dedicated to finding the monsters who killed his parents. And he would never give up hope of finding his sister.

He shook off the old memories when he heard Anthony Alessi's car finally pull into the driveway. "Do you have the key?" he called, getting out of his vehicle.

Anthony held up a key ring with a single key on it. "Yeah, got it."

Bishop saw the scowl on the other man's face as they both headed toward the front door. "Unlock it," the detective said. Alessi paused, glancing back over his shoulder before slipping the key into the lock, pushing the door wide, and stepping back out of Bishop's path. When the brother didn't follow him in, Bishop paused. "You coming?"

Without a word, Alessi crossed the threshold then stopped, staring up at the impressive staircase ahead of him. Bishop's eyes followed the other man's gaze. The beautiful hardwood certainly had its appeal, but he couldn't help thinking carpet might have spared the victim such severe injuries. Realizing Alessi was probably thinking about his brother lying at the bottom of those stairs, for the first time he felt compassion for Anthony. Big brother didn't appear as cocky or condescending standing there as he had at the hospital. Perhaps, Bishop thought, it's simply that he felt responsible for Freddie. Like he had to protect him.

The house was deadly quiet. No sound of a TV or music. When the two men locked eyes, it was Anthony who looked away first. He walked through the expansive downstairs with the detective following close behind. "Claire... Claire, are you here?" No answer.

"She must be upstairs," Anthony said heading for the staircase again.

"Makes sense, if she's that sick," Bishop answered. He followed Anthony who walked straight to the master bedroom. The covers were in disarray, but the bed was empty, and the open door of the en suite showed the same. A quick check found each room on the second level just as empty as the master. Bishop broke the silence. "Guess she must be feeling better, huh?"

"Maybe. Maybe we just missed her and she went to see Freddie."

"Why don't you give him a call? See if she's there."

"Yeah, sure. But wait, if she's not, that's going to upset him. Maybe I'll make a quick run over there and check."

"Yeah, go ahead, but I'm just going to take another look around first." Bishop headed back through the downstairs rooms, with Anthony tight behind him, and stopped in the kitchen. "Where does that door lead? The garage?"

"Yeah."

"That silver hybrid in the driveway is your brother's, so whose car is this?" Bishop asked looking from the car to the ashen face behind him.

"Claire," he said, barely above a whisper. "My God, where is she?"

A quick walk around the house and the rest of the property provided no answers.

"Now what?" Anthony asked.

"Now I need to widen the search. Can you think of anywhere else she might be? Anyone who might have picked her up and taken her to their place to look after her?"

Anthony shook his head. "She doesn't have any family in the area."

"What about friends?"

"Well yeah, she has lots of friends. I don't think she'd be staying with any of them, though. That doesn't sound like Claire."

"Maybe you don't know her as well as you think?"

"I think I know her a lot better than you, Detective."

There's the snide, condescending jerk I first met. Bishop headed back to his car.

"Now what?" Anthony called after him.

"Now I go talk to somebody who does know her... your brother."

"You're going to upset him, you know."

Bishop didn't miss the tremor in the other man's voice.

"Look, I'm not out to upset anybody, but like it or not, right now I've got a missing person to find." Without another word, Ron Bishop got in his car and took off leaving Anthony staring after him. The brother-in-law was not his concern. He was much more concerned about a woman with blonde hair—just like his Jane Doe—who was nowhere to be found. The question on his mind was simple. *Where are you, Claire Alessi?*

Ron Bishop pulled into the hospital parking lot and found a parking place. Staring at the entrance as daylight faded, his mind flew back to another time. Another person—a person he loved—who had simply vanished.

CHAPTER SEVEN

"Are you kidding?" Mia asked her roommate. "Dr. Gordon said he's discharging Freddie in two days?"

"Yep." Morgan looked back at the chart she was holding. "But he's gonna need a bed brought into their first-floor den. Apparently, he's in a two-story with all the bedrooms upstairs. Doc Gordon said his brother and the team will be helping him with all that."

After asking her roommate how Freddie felt about it, Mia went to check in with him personally. She wasn't too surprised to find Detective Bishop standing next to Anthony, but she was concerned about the tension filling the space and the scowl on her patient's face. Coming down the hall she'd heard their animated voices so it was obvious she was interrupting something.

"Should I come back later?" she asked.

"I think we're done here," Freddie said, head down, massaging his temples. When he raised his head again, Mia read the anguish in his eyes. She looked to Anthony for answers but saw none there. Freddie's voice brought her scrutiny back to him. "Find her!" His eyes went to the detective's. "Please," he said more quietly.

"We will, I promise. Anthony, I want to ask you a few more questions," Bishop said. Turning to Mia he added, "We'll get out of your way, Miss. And Freddie, we'll find her."

Mia watched the two men exit then turned her attention to her patient. But his attention wasn't on her. He looked almost catatonic.

"Freddie..." he jumped at the sound of his name. "Your wife? She still hasn't been in to see you?"

"She's missing, Mia."

"What?"

"They can't find her. They went to the house, but she wasn't there." His words poured out. "Nobody knows where she's gone."

"Well, do you think she's with a friend, or maybe a relative?"

"You don't get it. Her car is in the garage... and her keys. But not her phone. Where's the damn phone? Where's Claire?"

Mia reached for something to say. Some way to lessen his anguish. But she knew all too well how someone could disappear without a trace. But this wasn't about Mia's past, and his wife wasn't a silly teenager stupid enough to get in a car with a stranger. "Freddie, I'm sure they'll find her," she said taking the seat by his bed. "Why don't we talk a little about what you're going to do when you're discharged? And maybe you can do some drawing to calm yourself."

"What?" Freddie bellowed.

Mia knew by his tone, her words hadn't helped. She felt her own lack of experience. Self-doubt attacked.

"No," he said. "I don't feel like drawing any damn pictures! Is that going to find Claire?"

Mia had to admit, not everyone's drawings held secret messages. "I'm sorry, Freddie. It's all right. Of course you don't have to draw anything today. Let's just spend our time talking about what's next."

At the end of their session, which she'd shortened under the circumstances, she knew Anthony had agreed to stay with him for a few days if Claire wasn't home by then. And he was walking into his brother's room just as she was leaving.

"Oh hello, Anthony. About yesterday..."

"No worries," he said brushing past her and hurrying to Freddie's bedside.

Mia wasn't sure why his brusque response bothered her, but it colored her cheeks, and she turned quickly away, running smack into Ron Bishop.

"Whoa, what's your hurry... Miss Reed, right?"

"Yes, sorry, I was heading to my next patient and didn't see you there."

"Obviously," he said taking a step back.

Mia didn't care for the amusement in his eyes—since it was at her expense—but it was good to see the man could smile. The worry lines which had been so prominent before he'd left Freddie's room now smoothed out to reveal the bluest eyes she'd ever seen. She immediately thought again of her grandma's favorite actor, Paul Newman.

"So, do you know anything about Mr. Alessi's wife, Claire?"

His question jolted her back to the present and his now more serious countenance.

"No, not really," she replied. "Only that she's neglected to even visit her husband once. I guess that says a lot." Mia's family was the center of her world, so such neglect was incomprehensible.

"Well, Miss Reed, we don't know why she hasn't been in. There could be more to the story than we know." Of course, Mia thought. *Freddie said she's missing.*

***

Ron Bishop's gaze followed the art therapist until she passed the nurse's station and disappeared around the corner. She made him feel something. He wasn't sure what it was exactly, but he thought he liked it.

He shook it off and turned his attention to more important matters. He'd gotten a pretty good description of Claire Alessi from her brother-in-law, but he really needed a picture to circulate. He was sure Freddie would have one, but asking him would stir up more fear for the already shaken man. Better to go back to the house where he'd surely find what he needed.

On the drive back toward Bradford Woods, Ron's mind turned over the little information he had on the missing woman. One fact he couldn't escape... there was a Jane Doe lying in the morgue. And one thing he knew about her. She was a blonde.

Once back at the Alessi home, it didn't take long to find pictures of the missing woman. Definitely a blonde, and an attractive one at that. Her slight build was familiar too. Too familiar. *Hope I'm wrong.*

He really wanted his hunch to be incorrect. He hoped the Alessi woman had taken off somewhere—for whatever reason—and that she wasn't the one whose body they'd found early Tuesday morning. That's not the kind of news he wanted to take back to her husband.

Focus, Bishop. As much as he didn't want to know, he indeed had to, so he busied himself collecting the essential DNA, made the necessary phone calls, and headed to a meeting with the coroner.

CHAPTER EIGHT

It was nearly one o'clock when Mia finally had a break built into her schedule for lunch. By then she needed both the rest and the nourishment. She had just finished a session with her little group of Alzheimer's patients, and though she loved working with the three of them, it took a lot of emotional energy. At the end of their hour, she felt both gratified and drained. She took note of the time, grabbed her bag, and headed for the nurses' lounge to kick back for the next thirty minutes.

Rushing out the door, she nearly collided with Anthony. "Sorry," she said, "this seems to be my day for running into people."

"Excuse me?"

"Nothing, sorry," Mia said, moving to pass on his right. She was startled when she felt his hand grab her upper arm.

"Wait, don't hurry off." Mia's jaw dropped and Anthony let go of her. "I mean, please may I have a word with you?"

Mia took a deep breath and let anger chase away the panic coursing through her.

"Yes, I suppose, but I'm on my way to lunch so make it quick." As a rule she preferred not to be rude, but she needed these thirty minutes to refuel. And, after all, Anthony Alessi had brushed her off in their earlier encounter, hadn't he?

"I've got a better idea," he said. "Let me join you."

"I'm sorry, but it's employees only in the nurses' lounge. What did you need to talk about?"

"Please. Let me buy you lunch in the cafeteria."

"I brought my lunch today."

"Couldn't you save it for tomorrow?" At her hesitation he added, "Look, I don't know what I did to offend you, but whatever it was, I'd like to make it up to you." Tilting his head down to her level, he smiled and added, "Pretty please?"

Heat rose in her cheeks. Mia found it impossible not to melt looking into those big brown eyes. She glanced at her watch again. "Well, all right, but I'll have to keep an eye on the clock."

The walk to the cafeteria gave Anthony time to fill her in on what he and the detective had discovered at Freddie's house and how worried he was about Claire. Hearing the magnitude of his alarm, Mia understood why he had been so brusque when she saw him earlier. He was obviously worried sick, and telling Freddie must have been beyond difficult. No wonder Freddie had been so despondent during their session—too much to fill in all the details.

"You don't think something awful has happened to Claire, do you?" Mia asked setting her tray on the table. "I mean you don't think she was kidnapped or something... or do you?" The deep line between his brows said more than his words.

"I don't know what to think. I mean, I don't want to go there, you know?" He pushed his mac and cheese around on the plate then looked up. "And what about those texts she sent? If she's got her phone and she's texting, she must be okay, right?"

Mia's mind flashed back to those terrifying days she'd been locked up in a cage by unstable Benson and the text messages he'd sent her parents from her phone. But there was no need to worry Anthony more by suggesting such a possibility in this case. She avoided his question with a check of the time. "Oh gosh, Anthony. I'm sorry, but I've really got to get ready for my next patient," she said pushing her chair back.

"No, I'm the one who should apologize. I didn't mean to spend this time talking about Claire. Listen, let me take you to dinner and we'll just talk about you."

Mia laughed. "That would be a pretty short conversation," she said stalling while trying to decide what to do.

"Oh c'mon, I'll bet you're a lot more interesting than you give yourself credit. How about it?" Getting to his feet he added, "I won't take no for an answer. I'll pick you up at six."

"No," she said abruptly. Watching his face drop, she reached in her pocket for a pen and scribbled her address on a napkin. "I'll need time to get home and freshen up. Make it seven."

Hurrying away before he could object, Mia glanced back before walking out the cafeteria door. Anthony hadn't moved. He had a look on his face she couldn't quite read, but it didn't matter. Not until this moment had she realized she was excited by the prospect of having dinner with Anthony Alessi.

Mia was dressed and ready before seven o'clock even though she'd changed twice. She now wore the little black dress and pearls that once belonged to her mother... the mother she'd lost when she was a young child. She rubbed the jewels between her thumb and forefinger as she stared out the window.

A quick glance at her watch sent butterflies fluttering through her stomach. *It's 7:15. Where is he?* Self-doubt crept into her brain. She'd walked away after giving him her address and a different time. What if she'd turned him off?

Mia's relief was audible as his car pulled up and she let out the breath she hadn't realized she was holding. She darted back from the window before he could see her—sending Simeon scurrying into the solarium—and waited nervously pacing until she heard the knock on her door.

She stood for a moment, hand on the doorknob—she didn't want to seem too anxious—then slowly opened it. "Hi."

"Sorry I'm late, but you know traffic this time of day. Ready?"

"Sure," Mia said grabbing her clutch from the table by the door. He hadn't said a word about her appearance so she wasn't about to tell him how gorgeous he looked. "Where shall we go?"

"I made reservations at LeMont. I think you'll enjoy the view as well as the food."

Mia was shocked and impressed. She'd heard so much about LeMont on Mt. Washington and the amazing view, but she'd also heard enough to know she could never afford to go there on her tight budget.

She was surprised to hear Anthony greeted by name when they arrived. "Good evening, Mr. Alessi."

Once they were seated the sommelier quickly came to their table. "Good to see you again."

Anthony thanked him and selected a fine bottle of wine, looking to Mia only briefly for approval.

When it was time to order, he took charge and ordered for them both. Mia thought everything he chose sounded magnificent, but thought it somewhat presumptuous of him not to ask her first. What if she hadn't liked seafood? The lobster bisque would've been a big mistake. But she loved it. Almost as much as she loved the awesome view of Pittsburgh from where they sat.

By the time the waiter brought their entree—raspberry duck— Mia already felt like she'd been talking too much. But Anthony was so interested and wanted to know all about her. He showed special interest in what she did as an art therapist, and it made her feel good to be treated as a real professional. With some effort she put her mind to finishing her duck and the wonderful balsamic glazed asparagus and whipped sweet potatoes he'd ordered to go with it.

"So, how's it going with Freddie?" he asked casually as they walked to his car. "Do you think this art thing is helping him? I mean what exactly is it that you hope it will do for him?"

Mia didn't especially want to talk anymore about work, but she explained again how it could help people in general. "And I'm hoping it will help Freddie with his frustration over not recalling what happened Monday. Who knows? It might even help him remember." She changed the subject on the ride back to her place trying to learn more about him, and he explained—though she didn't really understand—all about his investment business. Still, she was impressed.

Back at her door, Mia wondered if he would ask for a kiss. Most guys did on a first date, she'd discovered. She pulled her key from her clutch and turned to thank him. "Thanks for a wonderful dinner. I really enjoyed it."

"I'm glad," he said, but he didn't ask if he could kiss her. He turned as though to leave, then abruptly turned back. He placed both hands behind her head, gently pulled her in to him, and firmly, slowly kissed her lips. "Goodnight, Mia," he murmured as he released her, and promptly left her standing alone.

Leaning back against the door, cheeks burning, Mia was stunned. She was breathless. But she knew one thing—she wanted more.

CHAPTER NINE

Mia stared at the file in her hands, but she didn't see the words on the page. She should be focused on the case, Freddie's case, but the image before her was another man. All she could see was Anthony's whiskey brown eyes. Closing her own eyes, she felt the warmth of his hands as he held her close... and the heat of his kiss... *Stop it!* Mia shook her head and refocused on the page in front of her. Freddie needed her full attention today.

He would be discharged in less than twenty-four hours, and Mia was determined to send him home in a better frame of mind. Today's session was not to be wasted.

"Good morning," she said with a sigh of relief. Freddie was alone. His brother wasn't there yet. *Maybe he didn't want to see me.* Mia chastised herself for being ridiculous and for again thinking of the wrong Alessi brother. She determined not to let it happen again. "How are you feeling this morning?"

Freddie's haggard face said more than his words possibly could. "Not great." He breathed in deeply and expelled the air before going on. "They haven't told me anything, you know. Anthony finally brought me my phone yesterday afternoon, for all the good it's doing me." His frustration was palpable. "Claire's missing, and I can't even look for her. I'm stuck in this bed." His fist pounded the mattress and his eyes pleaded for help.

Mia placed her hand over his closed fist. "I'm sure detective Bishop is doing everything he can. They'll find her, Freddie." She knew they were empty words, and she wasn't sure she believed them herself, but at least the muscles in his hand slowly unclenched.

He sighed, evidently resigned to the fact there was nothing he could do about it at the moment. Following only a few minutes of conversation—after all there wasn't much to be said that wouldn't add to his discomfiture—Mia suggested a move to the art room. She hadn't taken him there yet and hoped the change of scene might be enough of a distraction to diminish his depression.

When she wheeled him through the door, she saw his head turn from side to side taking in the vast amount of art supplies at hand. "I thought we'd try a different medium today," Mia said. "How about some watercolor pencils?"

"Sure, why not. How's that work?"

Not exactly an enthusiastic response, but at least he agreed to do something. That's the first step. Before long Freddie was engrossed in his task, and Mia watched the deep worry lines smooth. She led a light conversation, primarily about the watercolors they were using and comparing it to other mediums. In the back of her mind she looked forward to relaxing later, brush in hand, blending paint and water into something beautiful.

"I'm scared, Mia." Freddie leaned back into his wheelchair. "What if the guy who assaulted me did something to her? What if she's..." He paused, not wanting to finish the thought, but before he could, Mia rescued him.

"We don't know for sure that anything bad has happened to her. I mean, maybe there's a logical explanation." Mia searched for the words that might reassure him. "It all might make sense when she has a chance to explain." *If she gets a chance.* But Mia couldn't express such a thought out loud. She was there to relieve her patient's stress, not make it worse. She let her Pollyanna nature explore the more optimistic possibilities. "It may seem unlikely, but maybe she just decided to get away for a while for some reason."

The crease in Freddie's brow deepened. *Well, that's not good.*

Mia barely heard his next words. "Did she leave me?" Freddie spoke more to himself than to Mia, she was sure. His head lifted with a jerk. "She blames me, you know."

"Blames you for what?"

"The baby. We lost our baby." His chin dropped to his chest. "I should have been there." Freddie fell silent. The silence seemed like it would never end, but Mia had learned to force herself to wait.

When she could stand it no longer, she began, "Freddie..." She'd intended to ask him to explain, but his head popped up as though suddenly awakened from a dream.

"I wasn't home when she miscarried. I was playing golf with Anthony." The words came out in a rush. "Maybe if I'd been home, I could've gotten help quicker... I could've done something."

"No Freddie, don't do that to yourself." Mia took his shaking hand in hers. "I don't know exactly what happened with your wife, but I do know this. Most miscarriages are chromosomal anomalies." Seeing the puzzled look on his face, she went on, "I mean, like there's a missing chromosome. I know it's terribly sad... heartbreaking, but it's nobody's fault. Or did she have some kind of trauma, like a bad fall or car accident?"

"No, nothing like that. And the doctors told us about the chromosome thing, but I don't know if Claire bought it."

"Well it's true, and you've gotta stop beating yourself up. I'm sure there's nothing you could have done."

"But does she know that?"

"I'm guessing she does, Freddie."

"Then why would she leave?"

"I don't know. I never met her so I don't know what makes her tick."

"Well, I know her. Or at least I thought I did. She's my wife, for God's sake." Freddie gazed out the window. "I should have let her get it."

"Get what?"

"The mutt. She wanted to get this rescue, but I wouldn't hear it. No way," he said shaking his head.

"You're not a dog person, huh?" Mia said trying to keep up with his train of thought. She was bewildered by his reaction. Brows drawn together, he glared at her. Then she watched him take a breath and relax his jaw.

"No, I guess not... at least not anymore." Another deep breath. "We had a dog when I was a kid. Champ. I was about fourteen when somebody killed it."

"Oh no. That's awful!"

His eyes darted from Mia to somewhere across the room. "No, not after Champ, no more dogs for me, but..."

"It's okay, Freddie." Seeing his agitated state, she tried to reassure him. "I'm sure your wife wouldn't leave you over that."

Mia didn't like the increased stress she was seeing but knew if she tried to convince him Claire hadn't walked out on him, he'd focus on the uglier possibility that she'd been the victim of something much darker.

At the end of their session, which had run longer than intended and left Mia ten minutes behind schedule, she was relieved to find Freddie calmer. As she pushed his wheelchair into room 215, Mia was surprised to find Detective Bishop. Like a jack-in-the-box, he jumped up from one of the seats by the window and checked his watch.

"What is it? Did you find her?" Freddie asked.

Mia heard the fear in his voice, and she knew seeing the detective had chased all his calm away.

"I'm sorry, Mr. Alessi. I just came by to ask you a few follow-up questions about the day you were attacked." Bishop looked up at Mia. "They told me you'd be back from your session with Ms. Reed by eleven-thirty, so I waited."

Mia didn't care for his tone or the look he shot her way. She thought to tell him why they ran over—let the impatient detective know how important her work with Freddie was—but decided she didn't need to explain herself to this annoying individual. It was her turn to check her watch. "Do you want me to help you back into your bed, Freddie?"

"No, I'm gonna sit over there, and I think I can manage." With some difficulty, Freddie pushed himself up out of the wheelchair and dropped into a seat by the window. Normally, Mia would have dashed off to write her notes before having lunch and preparing for her next session, but she felt compelled to linger a while to be sure Bishop didn't undo everything they had accomplished in the previous hour.

"So, Mr. Alessi."

"Just call me Freddie, please."

"Okay, Freddie," Bishop continued. "Monday, the day you were attacked, you say your wife was at home?"

"Yeah, well, I mean, I think so." His hand grasped his jaw. "Schools were closed so she had the day off. She must've been home. Unless…"

As Freddie hesitated, Bishop's eyes landed on Mia. "Ms. Reed, were you finished with what you needed to do with your patient?"

Mia realized she was being dismissed. She didn't much like it.

"Freddie, if you need anything you can push your call button for Morgan."

Freddie wrinkled his brow then nodded and looked back to the detective who, pen poised over his notepad, continued to look at Mia. She backed out of the room and stood outside the door for a moment before forcing herself to move away. She tried to shake off her annoyance with the detective, but she didn't care for his dismissive attitude. She knew he had a job to do, and it was certainly crucial he find Claire, but his lack of appreciation for her role in helping Freddie was hurtful.

Regaining awareness of how far behind she was, Mia dashed down the hall. She knew by the time she charted her notes, she'd have a lot less time for lunch and to relax than usual. She had to allow ample time to prepare for her session with the small group of kids in pediatrics. Mia loved working with them, and although some of their conditions broke her heart, their positive attitudes and sense of humor brought a bit of joy and a beacon of light into her day.

Back in her office, Mia hit the keyboard. She included Freddie's reaction to finding the detective in his room, but her final thought—about Ron Bishop—didn't go on the screen. It stayed in her head. *He's a bit of an ass.*

She closed her laptop and headed for the door, hoping to salvage her lunch break and clear her mind. If she was lucky, she could still squeeze in a brief meditation before the chaos of the children.

She almost made it, but at the threshold she met an obstacle—the ass.

CHAPTER TEN

"Ms. Reed, do you have a minute?"

Mia looked at her watch, though she knew exactly what time it was. "What is it, Detective? I'm really running behind."

"Just a few questions. Won't take long."

Mia gave him a sigh filled with exasperation. "Yes, okay. But I don't know how I can be of any help." Moments later, she wondered why he had wasted his time asking her about Freddie's state of mind when he should have been out there looking for Claire Alessi. And she had made that very clear to him before walking away. "Don't you think his anxiety is understandable? I'm sure he'll be much better once you find his wife," she'd said with raised eyebrows.

"No, Ms. Reed. I wouldn't count on it," he'd said flipping his notebook closed. Bishop had turned and quickly walked away, throwing a "Thanks for your time" over his shoulder. But his tone hadn't assured Mia he appreciated her time at all. And what did he mean not to count on it? Did he know something she didn't, and were Freddie's worst fears going to be realized?

Mia rolled these thoughts around in her head as she mindlessly wolfed down her yogurt. The apple would have to wait until later. She had to take this moment to prepare for her kids. *Be present for your patient* had become her mantra, and right now that 'patient' was her little group from peeds.

Mia spread out the black, white, and assorted brightly colored poms, a variety of colored feathers, foam stickers and letters, and fuzzy sticks. She scattered some felt and velvet squares on the tables, then placed a stiff piece of paper on each of the tables where today's three patients would work on their soft projects. Her objective was not only for the kids to have fun and, at least for a little while, forget about needles, blood draws, and all the other discomforts of their hospital stays, but also to find comfort with the soft project they'd take back to their rooms.

As it turned out, only two patients showed up at the appointed time. Mia went to the door and looked down the hall. "Do either of you know where Tommy is?" she asked. Already seated at the tables, Amber shrugged as she stroked her cheek with one of the pink feathers.

"Maybe he got outta here," offered Hannah, reaching for letters and spelling out her nickname, Flash. She was one of the fastest girls in her school. Or she *had been* before she got sick.

Mia was about to explain the purpose of all the materials she'd laid out when Tommy rolled in with one of his nurses right behind. "Sorry, he's late, Mia. I brought him down as soon as he got back from x-ray," she said.

"No worries. He's just in time, thanks. Hi Tommy," she said. "Are you ready to get started?" Tommy nodded, but slumped in the chair. He didn't look especially enthused. Mia could only hope today's activity would lift his spirits. At ten, he was the youngest in this little group, while the girls were both twelve.

It didn't take long for all three children to become engrossed in their projects, and Mia watched as Tommy sat taller, choosing letters carefully. She was surprised when he lined them up, and she read the word "school." She had expected his name or home or some other word that signified happier days. But then she reminded herself, Tommy never talked about home. His mother spent as much time as she could with him, but Mia rarely saw his father. And she didn't like the vibe she got whenever she did.

Hannah had covered the top of her paper with the luscious blue velvet material and placed several yellow poms to make the sun. She cut yellow fuzzy sticks to make rays, and red letters spelled FLASH across the sky. She then cut green felt to represent grass and was gluing lots of red feathers in a row. They started on the bottom left and angled up into the sky by the time they reached the right side of the page.

"I love it," Mia said honestly. "What do the feathers represent to you?" The long pause that followed made Mia begin to think she shouldn't have asked.

Hannah looked out the window and slowly grinned. "Me," she said.

Mia's eyebrows shot up. "Oh, can you tell me more about that?"

Hannah's smile widened and she giggled before answering, "I'm running so fast, I'm running up into the sky."

Mia could see her patient was completely satisfied with her creation.

"Can I have an extra feather to take with me?" the girl asked.

"Sure you can," Mia said, happy to see such a positive outcome.

Amber's reaction wasn't as enthusiastic, nor did her picture tell a story. But Mia thought it had served its purpose all the same. Amber's paper had feathers glued at exact intervals along the edges and rows of pink and white poms in perfect horizontal lines. It was perfect and orderly. It was Amber. And with her project complete, she lightly rubbed her right hand over the soft poms.

Hanna, aka Flash, was the first to leave, waving over her shoulder and calling her goodbyes, and Tommy was right behind her. Mia heard Hannah suggest the candy-stripers who came to get them should race their wheelchairs to the end of the hall. Mia could only imagine the young volunteers' reactions but was quite sure they wouldn't dare comply... or would they?

"Amber, looks like it's just you and me. Wanna help me gather up some of these supplies?"

The girl nodded consent and slowly placed the colored poms in the right containers. Mia watched her careful placement of each box on the shelf, lining them up hesitantly so their edges matched exactly. Amber rarely spoke unless she was directly spoken to, so Mia was surprised when she heard the young girl's voice.

"Is that right?" Amber asked, glancing from the boxes to Mia and back again.

"Sure, there's no right or wrong way, sweetie, but they look perfect." She smiled at the child who returned a shy smile and Mia was certain she also saw relief sweep over her face.

Though anxious to clean up the studio, as a therapist she appreciated the opportunity to have a little one-on-one time with her quietest client.

"So, you didn't have much to share today," Mia said, knowing that was typical for this particular patient. "How's it going? Have they said when you'll be discharged?"

Mia noticed another slight change in the girl's expression. Her more serious demeanor was accompanied by a nod.

"Mom said I'll probably be able to go home in a couple days."

"You don't seem very excited about it. Don't you think you're ready?"

"Yeah, I guess, but..." Before Amber could finish her thought, her mom flew through the door.

"Hi hon, surprise!" Mrs. Mason hugged her daughter tightly. "I just got here, and your nurse said I could come down and get you." Amber's grin was the most animated Mia had seen. They both thanked Mia, but as they left, she heard Mrs. Mason say, "Your father will be in to visit after supper." Amber's face morphed once more, and Mia didn't like this latest expression.

The young girl didn't say much, but that look spoke volumes. This was not the look of a child happily anticipating a visit from her father. Mia couldn't help thinking of her own father and the wonderful relationship she had with him growing up... and still had. Not everyone was so lucky.

CHAPTER ELEVEN

At the end of a long day that ended an even longer week, Mia parked in the garage of her apartment building, but instead of heading upstairs, she locked her car and headed outdoors. She breathed in the fresh air of her favorite time of year and looked up at a clear blue sky. The sun warmed her skin without scorching it, and there wasn't the slightest hint of the sticky humidity summer would bring.

Pulling the phone from her pocket, she sent a quick text to her roommate. *Walking.* There was no need for more. Morgan knew her well enough to understand her need for time. Time to process. Time to quiet her mind. Time to find peace.

And she found it. For a while. Mia had learned to tune out the normal sounds of the city. She heard them only as a soft, blurred background of a bright, scenic panorama. Before long, though, her eyes looked inward. The focus on her breathing drifted to the events of the day. To her patients. Especially to Freddie and how he might handle the possible loss of his wife—whether she'd left him or worse. *Breathe. Focus on the breath. And Amber. Poor kid. Focus.*

The joyous sound of giggling girls pulled her attention from her mini-meditation. Three tweens—about the age of her afternoon therapy group—two sharing the conspiratorial tittering while one lagged quietly behind. The third girl looked nothing like Mia's patient, except for her facial expression. Mia immediately thought of Amber's somber demeanor. She shook off the memory, reminding herself the purpose of her late afternoon walk was to clear her mind. *Breathe.*

Moments later, another distraction—one she would normally be able to shut out—disrupted her inner quiet.

"For God's sake, hurry up!" a man called to his son, grabbing him by the arm and pulling him forward. The boy looked to his mother, but she returned a reassuring smile and didn't utter a word.

None of this was terribly unusual to see on the busy city streets, but it bothered Mia. There were too many things making her think of her young patient. She turned abruptly and headed back to the parking garage. Her faith and past experience had taught Mia to listen to her instincts, and right now she believed all signs were pointing the same direction. Though it might be ridiculous, she felt compelled to go check in on Amber Mason.

Back at the hospital, Mia's legs were tired so she hurried to the elevator rather than take three flights of stairs. The doors opened and a man pushed by her. Mia recognized the woman right behind him—who didn't acknowledge seeing her—as Mrs. Mason. A quick check of the time showed visiting hours weren't nearly over, but the Masons seemed in a hurry to leave.

Mia stepped on the elevator and pressed three, glad she had returned. "God, guide me," she prayed, and arriving on the third floor, she went directly to room #303. She found Amber, eyes downcast, stroking her cheek with one of the feathers she'd pulled from the corner of her soft project.

"Hi, Amber."

The girl's head shot up at the sound of Mia's voice, and she swiped away tears with the back of her hand. The puzzled look on her face was understandable. Mia had never gone to her patient's room in the evening before.

"How's it going?" Mia asked. Amber didn't answer immediately so Mia lied. "I just thought I'd check on you before I head home. You seemed kind of down today." That part was true.

"I'm okay," Amber mumbled.

Mia wasn't buying it. "I think I passed your parents leaving. Are they going to be coming back?"

"No, I don't think so."

"All right. Well, it's early," Mia said making a show of looking at her watch and settling in the chair between Amber's bed and the window. "How 'bout I visit with you a while?"

"Whatever." Amber's one-word answer, followed by sullen quiet, wasn't encouraging.

"Amber," Mia spoke softly. "I'm going to be honest with you. I'm a little concerned." No response. "I saw the expression on your face earlier today when your mom said your father would be in tonight." Still no reaction. "And you didn't seem excited about going home..." Seconds passed. "Sweetie, are you afraid of something... *someone*?" Amber's eyes flew to her therapist's face. All doubt was removed. Fear was written all over her face. "You know you can talk to me, don't you?"

Amber nodded. The silence that followed was deafening.

When Mia could abide it no longer, she said, "This seems really hard for you. If I'm reading this right... Amber, are you afraid of your father?" Mia saw the girl's eyes fill with tears, and when they escaped and slid down her cheeks, she dropped her chin and covered her face with her hands.

Mia grabbed a couple tissues from the box on the nightstand, handed them to Amber, and put a hand on her arm. "How can I help?" she asked. She hadn't encountered anything exactly like this and didn't want to overstep, but she knew she had a responsibility to help this child any way she could. "Do you want me to talk to him?"

"No!" Amber's response was so emphatic it bordered on panic.

"Okay, okay. Don't worry. But if you change your mind..."

"I won't. You'll only make it worse... just like *she* did." Amber's final words were spoken more to herself than her therapist.

"Who's she? Your mother?"

"No. My teacher. She came to the house and talked to them both, but it just made Dad mad. He went ballistic. Said it was none of her business. Everything was worse when she left."

"But I'm your therapist. If you tell me more about it, maybe I can reach him in a different way."

"No, it doesn't matter," Amber barked. "You'll just make it worse... just like I told her."

Mia saw the anguish on her patient's face. "Okay, Okay. I won't say anything to him without talking to you first."

"Yeah, my teacher said something like that, but then she showed up at our door."

"You can trust me, Amber."

"All right." She looked at Mia through searching, glassy eyes. "Promise?"

"Yes, of course," Mia said. "Why? Don't you trust me, Amber?"

"Well yeah, but I trusted her too."

"Who?"

"My teacher... Mrs. Alessi."

CHAPTER TWELVE

Ron stared at the computer screen in front of him. They hadn't found a single clue at the house. Now that the dead body in the morgue had been identified as that of Claire Alessi, forensics had combed the household looking for something, anything, that could help them identify who had ended this young woman's life.

Seemed she was well liked, a good teacher who cared for her students, a good wife, a good friend... so why? What was the motive? Who would want her dead? The thoughts chased each other around Ron's brain—but no answers came.

His superiors insisted all clues pointed to a break-in gone bad. Someone got caught in the act, fought with the husband and pushed him down the stairs, then killed the wife. And if it was a simple break-in gone wrong, what did they take? Or maybe it wasn't about theft at all.

But Ron wasn't buying it. He'd seen the corpse. Why would the perp leave Freddie Alessi lying there but move the woman's body? Take her to another location and dump her? And then there was the rage. If it was a common break-in, what made the culprit angry enough to cause that much damage?

Maybe it was some perv attacking the woman but the husband caught him, then they struggled, and Freddie lost. But Claire was the one who truly lost everything... even her life.

Ron jumped at the sound of his phone's vibration. He rarely had the ringer on. Too intrusive when he was interviewing possible witnesses. But in the deadly silence of his office in the precinct this time of night, even the buzz of the phone against his desktop was startling.

The voice on the other end of the line was also startling. He had no reason to expect a call from Mia Reed or an invitation to meet somewhere.

"I know it's late, and you may be off duty," she said, "but I have something I think I should talk to you about... it's about the Alessis." Ron leaned forward in his chair trying to get closer to whatever information she had.

"No worries, Ms. Reed. I'd be happy to stop by... or we could meet, have coffee, maybe at Zeke's? Do you know the place?" He had discovered over his years on the force, you could sometimes learn more face to face than over the phone. A person's expressions or body language shared more than their words. And they rarely lied as much.

Mia said she knew the place—stopped there occasionally on her way to the hospital—and twenty minutes later he drove down Penn and arrived to find her already seated, hands wrapped around a latte.

"Espresso?" the barista asked, glancing at the time.

"Sure," Ron answered, "and gimme some of those beans, too." He wasn't worried about the caffeine keeping him up. He knew sleep wouldn't be coming anytime soon. And popping a few of those chocolate-covered espresso beans might give him the boost he needed after a sleepless night. "Thanks for meeting me, Ms. Reed. I appreciate it."

"No, I should thank you, and call me Mia, please."

Ron searched her face for some kind of clue as to why she'd wanted to see him. He couldn't read her.

"Okay, so what's up, Mia? You said it had something to do with Freddie. Did he remember something?"

"No, I mean not that I know of. And I think he's still in a state of shock from learning of his wife's murder. This is something else." She looked into her coffee as though searching for words. Ron waited. "And maybe it isn't anything at all to do with him or his poor wife."

"You never know, Mia. Anything you can tell me, any detail, could be relevant, because honestly, we don't have any leads."

Mia filled him in on what she'd learned about Amber Mason's fear of her father and that she'd had to report her suspicions to Children's Services.

"You did the right thing. You didn't really have a choice," Ron reassured her. "But I don't understand what this has to do with the Alessi case."

"That's because I'm not finished."

Ron didn't miss the edge in her voice. Puzzled, he sat back in his chair and waited.

"When I asked the girl if she wanted me to talk to her father, she kind of freaked out."

"Yeah?"

"Yes, she said someone else had tried that, and apparently her father was infuriated. Amber said his temper's so bad, she thought he was going to hit her but he took it out on her mother."

"I still don't see what this has to do with me," he said growing impatient. But he clamped his lips shut when he saw the look he was getting from the young woman across the table.

Mia rolled her eyes and sighed deeply. "Maybe it doesn't have anything at all to do with anything... probably doesn't. It's just that the person who tried to talk to Mr. Mason was Amber's teacher, Claire Alessi."

Bam! Okay, so maybe it was a long shot, but Ron Bishop knew better than to dismiss it. He pulled out his notepad and scribbled down the info Mia had given him. "Do you have an address for the Masons?"

"Um, no, but the hospital would have it."

Ron saw the crease between her eyes deepen. He waited, wondering if she would share whatever was bothering her. Her next words explained it.

"Will you have to tell Mr. Mason I was the one who told you about all this?"

"No, no, not at all. I'll keep your name out of it if I can." He didn't think she looked reassured, and he could understand why. If this guy's temper was bad enough that Mia thought he could be involved in an assault and murder, she could be in danger if Mason found out she'd pointed a finger. There were no words needed for him to see her dread. "Mia, don't worry. Thank you... this could be important." Ron instinctively reached across the small table, and something stirred in him as he took her hand. "And I won't let anything happen to you."

"Yeah," she said, "Like they always say in the movies right before the witness is... eliminated."

Chapter Thirteen

Mia sat in the back of the church and watched as Freddie grabbed his crutches to follow Anthony, and other family members outside, but she hadn't missed the surprise in Anthony's eyes when he caught sight of her. She didn't plan to go to the cemetery and had no desire to intrude on the family's grief. She didn't even know why she was there, except she knew she had to be. Freddie looked older than he had just one week ago.

Following the crowd of mourners outside, Mia caught sight of Anthony standing by the vehicle at the front of the line. She felt something more than sympathy. They hadn't spoken, other than in passing, since they'd stood at her door and he'd pulled her close. Mia tried to shake off the memory of his lips on hers. This was neither the time nor the place to be having such thoughts.

Threading her way through the throng, Mia slipped back into her jacket and pulled it close against the chilly mist. She was amazed by the number of young people, most of whom were likely Claire Alessi's students, there with their parents. With reddened eyes, they embraced each other. Some were sobbing, their tears mixing with the light rain that had begun to fall. Others held their friends up. Losing a beloved teacher was hard in any case, but this wasn't a simple death. These young people had heard the news. They knew their teacher had been murdered, and Mia could see their struggle to understand, to accept, to cope.

She stopped short when she saw Amber with her parents and a younger child. Mia put up her hand to wave, then quickly withdrew it after glancing at the girl's father. That's when she noticed Mr. Mason looking her way.

Turning quickly, Mia continued to her car, anxious to get as far away from the Masons as possible. Ever since she'd shared her concerns, her suspicions, with Detective Bishop, she had been anxious. Who knew how this man might react if he found out she was the one who'd called Children's Services, or worse yet, talked to the police? She was about to hop in her car when a man's hand grabbed her by the arm. Nearly jumping out of her skin, Mia spun around and found herself looking into those big brown eyes.

"I'm glad I caught you." From a distance Mia hadn't noticed how tired Anthony looked. "What's wrong? I didn't mean to startle you."

"No, it's okay. How are you?" Mia realized that was a stupid question as soon as she said it. "I mean, I'm so sorry. For you and Freddie. I can't imagine what you're going through."

"Thank you. I appreciate it. Are you leaving?"

"Yes. I didn't mean to intrude."

"Don't be ridiculous. You're not intruding. I know you care about my little brother."

Mia wondered if he knew she also had a crush on big brother.

Anthony glanced back at the vehicle way in the front of the growing caravan that would likely stretch for a mile. "Listen, I've got to get back to Freddie..."

"Of course," Mia interrupted. "You should go."

"Yes, yes, I should but... I... I... Can I call you?"

Mia let go of the breath she'd been holding and nodded. "Of course. And let Freddie know he's in my prayers. You all are."

She jumped in her car and started the engine, though she wasn't sure she could get off the lot until the entire line of cars going to the cemetery had left the church. When she was sure Anthony would have moved on, she looked out the window. With perfect timing, it was at that moment he looked back over his shoulder. And flashed a smile.

Mia lowered the window. She needed some air to cool the fire blazing in her cheeks.

When the church parking lot finally emptied enough to pull out, Mia heard another car engine and looked into the vehicle across from her. She hadn't expected to see Det. Ron Bishop.

***

The apartment seemed to whisper, *"You are alone."* Mia usually enjoyed the solitude of her little home away from home that she had made with her roommate. But staring out the window at the fading light, all she felt tonight was alone. Even stroking Simeon's silver fur couldn't chase the loneliness away. She missed her family. She especially missed her sister, Julie. They hadn't been born sisters, but after their parents married and they became step-sisters, a bond had developed and the 'step' was forgotten.

Mia took a deep breath, grabbed her phone, and shot off a message to Julie. *Busy?*

The reply came almost instantaneously. *No. What's up?*

What's up was too much to text, so Mia hit Facetime.

"Hey little sister, what's going on?" Julie said. And Mia's mood lifted just seeing her sister's sweet smile.

"Not much, but missing you guys." Mia choked back tears, took a breath and said maybe moving so far away was a mistake. She thought she'd gotten past being homesick halfway through her first year at Seton Hill, but here it was again.

"C'mon Mia, what happened? I haven't seen you like this in a long time."

Mia quickly brought Julie up to date on her latest client and his wife's demise. And Julie had lots of questions. She ended with, "Do they have any suspects?"

"I'm not sure. I mean there is only one person I know who maybe had a grudge against her, but I'm not sure he could've done this. It seems like everybody loved her. You should've seen the crowd at the funeral today. Her students were devastated."

"You went?"

"Yeah, I never met her, but her husband was my client... and his brother is..." Mia searched for words to finish her sentence.

Julie sucked in her breath. "You like him! Oh my gosh, why haven't I heard about him before?"

Mia laughed and knew she was blushing. "Well, we've only been out once."

"Holy macaroni! You're dating him?"

"Well, like I said, just the one time."

"That's it. I think it's time for a big sister visit and sleepover. Okay?"

Mia couldn't think of any better medicine. "This weekend?"

Julie promised to be there sometime Friday night—possibly by nine. Ending the call, Mia sank back into the brown beast with a big grin on her face. She didn't think the night could get any better. That is until her phone rang and she recognized the caller ID. She hadn't expected his call tonight. Not the night of his sister-in-law's funeral.

"Hello, Anthony."

CHAPTER FOURTEEN

A three-minute phone conversation and Mia's mood soared. It hadn't occurred to her she would see Anthony so soon, but he said he'd be there in about twenty minutes. No time to shower again, but she could make a quick change of outfit, freshen her makeup, and comb her hair.

By the time she'd pulled herself together, there was a knock at the door. Blowing the air out of her lungs, Mia checked herself in the mirror and opened the door. She was about to say how glad she was to see him but never got the chance.

Anthony pulled her to him and kissed her long and hard. Mia feebly tried to pull away, but he held her fast, and she felt herself submitting... then joining, not wanting the kiss to end. She was lost in lust as the heat rushed from her lips to every cell of her body. With her world spinning, she lost her balance when their lips parted and he finally loosened his hold. Anthony caught her, held her up, and whispered, "I'm sorry."

Mia was speechless. She knew she should be enraged by the audacity of his actions. She should have slapped his face, told him off... something. But all she wanted to do was fall back in his arms. She could think of nothing to say and stood motionless staring into those dark, mysterious, brown eyes.

"Mia, sweet, sweet Mia. I had to see you."

"But the funeral. Your brother?" Mia said taking a step back and reaching for time to think. Time to compose herself. "Shouldn't you be with him?" Knees still weak, she turned toward the sofa to have a seat, but Anthony grabbed her elbow hard.

He quickly let her go when she flinched. "Damn it! I'm sorry... I don't know what's wrong with me. Freddy's fine," he said. "Our parents are with him. Trust me, they'll take care of their baby."

Surprised by what she read as bitterness in his voice, Mia quickly moved to the sofa and waited.

"Listen," he said, "you know I'd do anything for my little brother, but with them in town, he doesn't need me. Besides, right now I just need you."

Her defenses crumbling, Mia suddenly felt quite vulnerable. But how well did she know this man? And here they were alone in her apartment. Red flags flying, she perched on the edge of her seat ready for flight—but torn between flying to the door or flying into his arms.

"Mia, you're shaking... Are you afraid of me? You look like a swimmer who's seen a shark." Anthony held both hands up as though under arrest. "Of course, you must think I'm mad. The way I came in here and... listen, let's start over." He moved slowly now, taking a seat on the opposite end of the couch. "It's been a rough day. A heartbreaking day. And when I saw you at the church, well, you were like a little bit of sunshine on this otherwise truly gloomy afternoon." He paused, looking down at his hands. Mia saw the white-knuckled grip they had on each other. "Honestly, I couldn't stop thinking about you... and I had to get away from all the anger and sadness in that house. Can you forgive me for being such a jerk?"

"You're not a jerk, Anthony." Mia's heart softened seeing the forlorn look on his face. "You just took me by surprise." It was true. He had startled her. But she couldn't deny how her body had responded to his kiss. To his touch. "You said something on the phone about grabbing a bite to eat. So... so why don't we do that?"

They passed Morgan on the way out, and Mia told her she should be back in about an hour.

"Maybe a couple of hours," Anthony called back as they continued out of the building.

All right, a couple of hours sounds good to me, Mia thought.

Anthony asked if she was okay with pizza then drove to Pizzaiolo Primo, another place she'd never eaten. But the casual dining atmosphere was more what she was used to, and the prices closer to an intern's wallet. Looking over the menu, Mia wasn't sure where to begin—it all looked so good and she was suddenly famished—but she needn't have worried.

"I know just the thing if you're looking for comfort food, and I know I am," Anthony said. "Let's start with an antipasto and then do the ravioli. They use the freshest ricotta. You'll love it."

Mia thought that sounded perfect, and she wasn't wrong.

As they chatted their way through the meal, she was fascinated by their ability to have such mundane dinner conversation while her brain insisted on replaying their earlier encounter in the background. She wondered if he was thinking about it too. She couldn't tell. He didn't seem quite the same man sitting quietly across the table asking about her job, her family, her interests outside of work. It wasn't until later she realized he was still a complete mystery.

But it didn't matter. She didn't care. Mia only knew she didn't want her time with Anthony to end. They lingered over the delightful latte and when their cups were drained, Anthony pulled back her chair as she stood. Then he placed his hand on her back, guiding her toward the door. That simple touch made her heart thump harder, and once back in his midnight-blue Tesla her heart sank. She didn't want the evening to end.

"Do you mind if we go for a little drive?" Anthony asked. "I really don't want to take you home yet... and I'm certainly not anxious to go back to my brother's place. Not yet."

Mia agreed, wondering if he had read her mind.

The overcast day had cleared to unveil a perfect, star-filled sky with a full moon screaming romance. And when Anthony pulled into a scenic overlook, the spectacular view of the city took her breath away. It was all simply too perfect. Like a fairy tale, she was Cinderella sitting there in the coach with her Prince Charming.

"Mia..."

Hearing her name, she snapped back to reality, chiding herself for such foolishness. She turned to him expectantly.

"Do you forgive me?"

"For what?" she asked.

"You know. Back at your place... I guess I got a little ahead of myself."

"There's nothing to forgive," Mia heard herself say. Her heart jumped when he reached across the console and took her hand. Then as quickly as he'd taken it, he let it go, jumped out of the car, and dashed around to her side.

He pulled her out, and ignoring the few people in their cars nearby and the cool night air, took her in his arms once more. But instead of kissing her like she'd thought he was about to, he just hugged her tight... so tight it took her breath away and she no longer noticed the chill.

When he loosened his hold and peered down at her, Mia tried to read his eyes. They were happy. Definitely happy. But something more. Something she couldn't quite read. And something she quite forgot about when he lifted her chin and she finally felt the fervor of his kiss.

CHAPTER FIFTEEN

Ron tossed his cell on the desk, rocked back in his chair and wondered why she didn't answer her phone. Ever since he'd seen her at the church parking lot earlier in the day, Mia had been on his mind. "It's just as well," he said to no one. Nobody else in the precinct was nearby, and he wondered why he was still there.

Trying to shake off the memory of the young woman haunting his thoughts, the detective turned his focus to his most important case. He spread out the pictures of Claire Alessi—the one of an attractive young blonde as well as the gruesome images of the victim whose body they'd found. It was hard to believe it was the same woman. He slid the grisly images under the one of Claire Alessi laughing up at her husband. They looked so happy. And someone took it all away.

Ron Bishop was determined to find out who did it and bring them to justice. The idea of the murderer—any murderer—still being out there living their life when they'd destroyed so many others made his blood boil.

He slammed the Alessi file closed and reached across his desk to grab the pictures in the double frame. The one on the left, his parents' wedding photo, the other of his twin sister, another blonde. He stared at the pictures wishing they could dull the aching inside. Hoping they'd replace the horrific image of that night he'd found his parents dead in their living room and no sign of his sister. She'd vanished, leaving a void in his life... he hung onto the hope she was still alive out there somewhere.

Minutes slipped by while he was lost in the past, until the hum of his phone roused him from his melancholy memories. "Yeah," he snapped into the phone without first checking the caller ID.

"Is... is this Detective Ron Bishop?" the voice said timidly.

The detective thought he recognized the caller but had to be sure. "Yes, this is Bishop. Who's this?"

"Mia, Mia Reed... Freddie Alessi's art therapist. I saw that I missed a call from you?"

Ron frantically searched for how to respond. Why had he called? And what had he planned to say? "Uh, yeah, Miss Reed, I mean Mia," he corrected remembering what she'd said when they met at Zeke's. "I, um, I wanted to know if you'd heard anything more from the Mason girl."

"No, she was discharged," Mia said sounding surprised by the question.

"Oh, right. Well, um, anything new from Alessi, I mean Freddie, or his brother?" He had seen Anthony follow her to her car. Saw them speaking. *What were they talking about?*

"No, Detective. I've told you everything I know, which isn't anything really..."

"Okay, right. I understand. But if you hear anything, or think of anything—no matter how small—please give me a call. You never know. Even the tiniest detail might help."

"Of course." There was a pause. He could think of nothing more to say. "Is there anything else?" she asked.

"No... no, but thanks. And just call me if you think of anything." *You just said that, fool.* He stared at the phone in his hands but saw the face of a girl he couldn't get off his mind. Mia.

CHAPTER SIXTEEN

"I'm sorry," Mia said. "I thought it might be something important."

"What did he want?" Anthony asked. They were back in the car, but he hadn't started the engine.

"Nothing important. He just wanted to know if I'd heard anything that might help with your brother's case."

"Why would you? Why is he asking you?"

"It's no big deal, Anthony," she said noticing how his eyes squinted in questioning. "It's just that another patient had told me something he thought might be relevant."

"Who was that? What did they say?" he asked drumming his fingers on the steering wheel. Not at all warm herself, Mia was surprised by the beads of perspiration on his forehead.

"Well, that's confidential. I can't really share what other patients have told me."

"But we're talking about my brother's wife. I think I have a right to know."

Mia's jaw dropped at the sudden, drastic change in his mood. But she took a breath. Tried to understand. Of course he'd want to know.

"I'm sorry, Anthony. I wish I could tell you, but really, I don't know anything that would help." She wasn't sure if that was completely true. Maybe the connection between Mason and Claire Alessi was relevant. But perhaps it wasn't. Just because he had a bad temper and was probably a bully and abuser, didn't make him a murderer. Mia watched Anthony drumming his fingers on the steering wheel. "Maybe if you want more information, you could check with Detective Bishop," she said. "I know he's following every lead."

"Like what? What did he say?" Anthony stared at her hard. She wished he would blink.

"I said I don't know." Mia knew by the look on his face, Anthony heard her annoyance.

"Okay, yeah, I'm sorry." He looked so miserable Mia couldn't be angry with him.

"Hey, no worries. But I think we'd better head back to my place." Mia made an obvious show of checking her phone for the time. "It's getting late."

Anthony started the Tesla and pulled out, leaving the magic behind.

His sullen mood didn't lift on the ride back until Mia broke the silence, thanking him for dinner. A smile lit his face like a shade had been drawn to let in the morning sun. The change was so sudden it startled her. So did his next words. "Okay, we're here. We'll have to do this again sometime."

He didn't move to get out of the car, and Mia puzzled about what to do next.

When she didn't move to get out of the car either, he added, "I really have to get back and check on Freddie, okay?"

"Sure thing." As she reached for the door handle, Anthony finally bolted out of the car and ran around to let her out. He saw her safely inside the apartment then left without so much as a little peck on the cheek. *What the heck?*

Back inside, Mia scooped up Simeon, flopped onto the brown beast and thought back on the events of her rollercoaster day. She had to laugh when Morgan popped out of the bathroom wearing her charcoal mask. Simeon even stopped purring and stared in bewilderment. The perfect distraction. "Looking good, roomie."

"Never mind that, little girl. I've got fifteen minutes. Fill me in?"

"Fill you in about what?" Mia teased. She'd gotten used to her roommate calling her "little girl," and she knew it was meant with love, but she had to give her a hard time for it.

"You know what," Morgan said from the desk chair she'd perched on. "Don't make me come over there and shake it out of you... or kiss you and share my beauty mask."

"No, no, not that." Mia took a breath. "There's not much to tell really. We had a very nice dinner—Italian—delicious actually."

"And?"

"And what?"

"Oh, c'mon. You've been gone for hours. And even you don't eat that slowly."

Mia laughed. She didn't really want to talk about it, but she knew Morgan wasn't going to let her off the hook until she gave her something. "Okay, so we went for a little ride after."

"And?"

"And nothing," Mia said. "We talked. He brought me home." She shrugged. "That's all."

Morgan frowned, obviously expecting more.

Then Mia remembered the phone call. "Oh, and that detective called. He wondered if I knew anything more that might help find who killed my patient's wife."

"How would you know any more about it than he already knows?"

"I'm not sure. I've told him everything I can think of. Now, you better go get that black stuff off your face before it becomes permanent."

"Oh, don't you worry. My Mary Kay mask is keeping me gorgeous."

Mia grinned as she watched her roommate sachet back to the bathroom. Since they'd moved in together, their friendship had grown until they were like sisters. That thought took Mia back to her earlier conversation with Julie, the sister she'd been gifted with as a child. She couldn't wait to see her. Maybe Julie could help figure out the enigma that was Anthony.

CHAPTER SEVENTEEN

Mia rushed home from the hospital, made reservations for dinner with Julie, and with at least another hour before her sister would arrive, grabbed her sketchbook to help pass the time. She had no plan. Nothing specific in mind to draw. So she began with doodles and watched it slowly evolve. Clouds appeared as her pencil lightly danced across the paper adding more and more detail. Soon there was a house. A house surrounded by cars. Her hand was no longer her own as the pencil flew, etching the final details until Mia stopped, slowed her breathing, and looked at the picture her hand had crafted.

Indeed it was her hand, but she was certain it was not her consciousness that had created the image before her.

A thought came to mind, and she scrolled through the pictures on her phone. No, it wasn't the same house. As was her habit, Mia had taken a shot of the watercolor she'd done at the hospital—the one of Freddie's house. She compared it with her latest sketch, but there was very little resemblance. No, it wasn't the same house. She noticed two of the cars surrounding the house resembled police cars. And she knew these pictures—the ones that seemed to come from some other source—usually had a special meaning. *But what does this one mean?*

Mia jumped and ran to the door at the sound of her sister's familiar knock, sending Simeon dashing to one of his favorite hiding places in Mia's bedroom.

Mia and Julie embraced for their traditional "I love my sister" hug. The tradition had begun when they were in first grade and started getting into lots of squabbles they'd never had before. Their mom would give them a five-minute timeout, then the girls had to hug and say "I love my sister" five times before being allowed to play. It usually started off begrudgingly and ended with giggles.

What had begun as part of Mom's discipline, had fallen by the wayside until the first time they were separated—the time Mia had been kidnapped and Julie was terrified she'd never see her again—and when they were reunited, Mia heard Julie whispering through tears, "I love my sister," over and over again as they embraced. It was now the way they always greeted each other after any extended separation. And they still ended in giggles.

"All right, little sister, what's going on? Tell me everything," Julie said. "And what's this new boyfriend of yours look like?"

"Oh my gosh, Julie, he's not my boyfriend. And besides, that sounds so high school. But you know what? We went for a ride last night after dinner, and I got him to do a selfie," Mia said grabbing her phone. "I know he probably thought I was silly. He's a little older and most likely considered it childish, but I couldn't help myself." She flipped the phone around for Julie to see and watched her sister's jaw drop as she put both hands over her heart. "I know, right?" Mia said.

"Are you kidding? He's gorgeous! And he looks so sophisticated. How old is he anyway?"

"Well, I never asked him, but remember, his brother's my patient, and I know from his chart that Freddie's twenty-seven. And now I remember he mentioned once that Anthony was five years older, so..."

Julie did a quick calculation. "Thirty-two! An older man," she said arching her eyebrows and falling back into the seat cushions, eyes still wide. "Oh, there you are, Simmie," she said when the cat meandered into the room and wandered over to his tower, jumping easily to the top. "Yeah, that's right, just ignore me." Seeing that Simeon was doing just that, Julie turned her attention back to Mia. "Okay, hot-stuff, so tell me about this date last night."

"It wasn't really a date."

"You had dinner, right?" Mia nodded. "And then you went for a ride? Okay, you can call it whatever you want, but it sounds like a date to me. Whatever. So how did it go?"

Mia couldn't help smiling when she thought about it. "Okay, so dinner was delicious. He ordered for me. He seems to like to do that. Then, like I said, we went for a ride up to where we could look out over the city. It was gorgeous."

"You should see your face," Julie interrupted. "You don't have to tell me if you liked it. So then what? Did you kiss him? I know you kissed him."

"I think it would be a little more accurate to say he kissed me." Mia could feel the heat rising in her cheeks as she remembered the warmth of his kiss.

"Oh, I know that blush," Julie said. "You definitely like him. So then what happened?"

"Nothing really. I got this phone call from Detective Bishop, and I guess it kind of broke the mood because Anthony started asking me all these questions I couldn't answer, then he just brought me home."

"Wait, what?" Julie was interrupted by Mia's phone signal. She mouthed she was going to the bathroom, and Mia took the call.

"Hello?" Mia said, though she knew exactly who it was. Anthony's lighthearted tone was somewhat surprising after his rather sullen mood the night before.

"How about I come pick you up and we'll grab some dinner?"

"Oh no, I can't tonight."

"Why not?" Anthony's tone was no longer as light and friendly.

"I already have dinner plans."

"Oh, I see. Well, okay then." The call ended abruptly.

"Who was on the phone?" Julie asked returning from the bathroom. "Are you okay?"

Mia tilted her head. "I think so, yeah. That was Anthony. He asked if I wanted to grab something to eat, but I told him I already had dinner plans tonight."

"Well, that's good. You don't want to be too available." She gave her sister a wink and asked, "So where are we going?"

"I made reservations at that Italian place where I told you I had dinner with Anthony last night. I know you love Italian, and the menu had something I'd really like to try." Mia had enjoyed what Anthony had ordered for her the night before, but she looked forward to picking her own meal tonight.

"Is that your sketchpad on the desk? Have you been drawing pictures of your new beau?" Julie teased, crossing the room to take a look.

"No, just a house. And he's not my beau."

"Oh, this looks like one of your special ones, right?" Julie said. Over the years Mia's sister had learned to recognize the slight differences between her typical art and the ones they called *special*... the ones they had learned were inspired from another power.

"Yes, it seems God is trying to tell me something again, but I have no idea what it is." Mia took the tablet from her sister, gazed at the picture, then tossed it back on the desk. "I guess He'll tell me when it's time. We'd better get going if we're gonna make our reservation."

Once at the restaurant, all thoughts of drawings and boyfriends were forgotten as two sisters traveled back in time reminiscing and laughing about childhood shenanigans and their brothers' mischievousness. It was hard to believe, Cody would be graduating from Penn State in June, Bobby would be a senior at Westchester, and little Destiny was almost a teenager.

Julie, who still lived in their hometown near their family and old friends, was catching her sister up on everyone, but Mia was no longer listening.

"Mia, did you hear what I said?"

"Oh, um, yes, but..." She didn't get to say anything more before the tall familiar man stopped at their table.

"Why hello, Mia. So you must have enjoyed your dinner last night," he said stealing a quick glance at her dinner partner then looking back at her. Mia introduced him to her sister, then he apologized for the intrusion and went downstairs where it was more casual.

"Holy macaroni! He's hot!" Julie said in a stage whisper.

"Yeah, he is." Mia smiled. *But what is he doing here? AND why was he up here if he planned to eat downstairs?* She thought it was ridiculous to be suspicious, but couldn't help wondering... "I'd think maybe he was checking to see who I was having dinner with," she said, "but that's silly. I didn't tell him where we were going. I guess he really likes this place. But what a coincidence."

CHAPTER EIGHTEEN

Mia awoke to a familiar pawing on her back, the smell of coffee, and the warmth of sunshine coming through the window. As she was more of a tea drinker, it wasn't the scent of coffee that pulled her from her bed though. It was the delightful sound of her sister's laughter mingling with that of her roommate that prompted Mia to dash to the bathroom and brush her teeth so she could join the merriment.

It had been a long while since she'd spent time with Julie—not since she'd gone home for Christmas. She'd stayed in the Pittsburgh area for Easter and gone to church with Morgan, but had missed spending that special time with her own family, missed their Easter morning greeting—"Christ is Risen"—and the response—"He is risen indeed." Her parents' God-centered marriage had laid a strong foundation for Mia's beliefs, and her own gifts and revelations made her faith unshakeable. But at this moment her mind wasn't on her religious beliefs. She simply didn't want to waste another minute hanging out in bed when she could be spending time with Julie.

"Good morning, ladies. Is this a private party or can anyone attend?" Mia asked finding her roommate and sister at the kitchen table.

"Good morning, sleepyhead," Julie said. "I thought you'd wake up when I got outta bed, but you were sleeping like a brick."

"Yeah, that's the best I've slept in a while. You must've worn me out gabbing last night."

Mia brewed her tea and thoroughly enjoyed the camaraderie for the next half hour. She was sipping her second cup when Morgan dragged herself from the table where they'd all gathered.

"Guess I'd better mosey on outta here. Marcy was on last night, and I'm sure she wouldn't appreciate me coming in late," Morgan said reaching for her bag and heading toward the door. "Maybe next time you come out won't be a weekend I'm working, and I can hang with you longer," she said to Julie.

After their quick goodbyes, Mia had to admit she was happy to have her sister all to herself again. They spent the morning lazily reminiscing before Julie approached the subject of Anthony and his family again. Mia filled in the details and brought her sister up to date with all she knew, then remembered the drawing she'd done of Freddie's house.

"You said you wanted to see where I work. Why don't we go to the hospital, and I'll show you? We can even have lunch in the hospital cafeteria," Mia said tongue in cheek.

Julie rolled her eyes. "You're going to have to do better than that, sis."

Mia said goodbye to Simeon, then almost as an afterthought, grabbed her sketchpad. After stopping for burgers, she led her sister into the hospital and showed her around the art room on the way to her office. She was relieved to find they were alone when they got there, and went straight to the watercolor she'd done of Freddie's place.

"You see, the car in the garage in my painting is definitely blue... like Freddie said the one in his painting was even though that one was a pencil drawing," Mia said. "Do you think him saying it planted the idea in my head and that's why I painted it blue?"

"I don't know, Mia. I mean that makes sense, but you know more about what goes on in your brain with these drawings than I do."

"You'd think so, huh?" she said scratching her head and staring hard at her creation.

"What's that supposed to be?"

Mia looked where her sister was pointing. *What is that?* There was something blue on the ground near the entrance to the house. Moving closer to study the detail, she finally recognized what looked like a piece of jewelry. "I think maybe it's an earring. That's so weird. I don't remember painting that."

"Have you shown this to that detective?"

"No, why? Do you think I should?"

"Well, what do you think?"

"Yeah, I guess you're right, Jule. He'll probably think I'm crazy though. And he can be very annoying."

"How do you mean?"

"I'm not sure exactly. Well, he's like so abrupt and he thinks everybody else should get out of his way while he does his thing. Yanno?"

"I guess," Julie said. And seconds later, "But he's trying to solve a murder, right?"

"Yes, I know. And why are you looking at me like that?" She recognized the look on her sister's face. She'd seen it before—every time Mia went off course, Julie would give her that look. It was infuriating... but it always made her stop and think. "Oh, all right. I know what you're thinking."

"You do?" Julie said with a sly look on her face.

"Yes, you. I guess I'll show him... but I still say he'll think I'm a simple-minded child with my silly drawing."

"Well maybe, but you never know. And this might be important. I know you," Julie said putting her arm around her sister.

Mia agreed to call Detective Bishop but decided it could wait. Right now she and her sister had a beautiful day to enjoy and possibly a mall to visit.

Once they'd left the hospital and were walking to the car, Mia remembered the sketchbook she'd carried inside. "Oh nuts, I meant to compare the picture I drew yesterday while I was waiting for you to the one of Freddie's house."

"We can go back," Julie offered.

Mia thought about it but decided it wasn't necessary.

"I'll look at it Monday, and I know it's not the same house. I just wondered if there were any similarities." Mia breathed in deeply then added, "Let's just enjoy the day. You know it's not my only sketchpad."

CHAPTER NINETEEN

The weekend had flown by for Mia, and after the usual tearful goodbye with Julie right after Sunday morning's church service, she'd called and left a message for Detective Ron Bishop to please call her the next day.

It wasn't until she got up Monday morning that she realized there was a missed call on her phone. The message had been left at nearly midnight so with her phone on silent and Mia having been asleep by eleven, it went unheard.

Det. Bishop's voicemail was short and to the point. *"Sorry to call so late. Uh, yeah sorry. I'll try you tomorrow."*

He'd also sent a text one minute later indicating he'd just gotten back from a crime scene and then he apologized again.

The detective was as good as his word. Luckily, at seven-thirty in the morning, Mia was still in her office reviewing notes on morning patients when she got the return call.

"Hello, Detective," she said.

"Yeah, hello. Sorry about last night. Hope I didn't wake you."

Mia assured him he hadn't.

"So, what's up? Something about the Alessi case?"

"Well, maybe. I mean, it may be nothing..."

"Let me be the judge. What is it?"

"It's just something in a couple of drawings," Mia said.

"Drawings?" He sounded bewildered.

Mia was even more certain he'd think she was nuts and began doubting herself. She wanted to give Julie a shake for suggesting this, but now she had to follow through.

"Yes, Detective. Drawings," she said defensively. "You might remember I'm an art therapist. And... and, well there's a chance there's maybe something here that can be helpful to your investigation." Trying to sound as professional as possible, Mia's confidence still dwindled.

After an uncomfortable pause, Bishop finally responded that he'd come take a look. "Give me about an hour. You're at the hospital?"

"Yes, but I won't be available then. Can you make it around noon?"

"Yeah, all right. Noon then." And he abruptly ended the call. Again, Mia was offended by his curt tone. *Ass.*

However, it was time to be present for her patients. Ron Bishop got pushed to the back of her mind so she could do just that. Mia's dementia patients were so special to her, and she often thought of her Grandma Val's best friend—the one she'd always called Aunt Bonnie—who was the same age as many of her patients, but still sharp as a tack. As she looked at her favorite patient in the group, Lillian Perry, Mia decided she must send Aunt Bonnie a nice newsy letter soon.

It wasn't until the last of her Alzheimer patients was being wheeled back to her room that Mia checked the time and hurried from the art room to her office. She was surprised to find Ron Bishop leaning in the doorway when she got there.

"Detective," she said curtly before reminding herself he was here at her request. "Thank you for coming over."

"Sure thing. So, let's see these pictures."

"Right." Mia first grabbed Freddie's drawing and handed it over.

"Okay, looks like the Alessi house," Ron said after studying the drawing for a few seconds. He raised his eyebrows in query.

"That's right," Mia replied. "Freddie drew this in one of our first sessions." Seeing Bishop tilt his head, looking like her family dog asking for a treat, she continued. "What was kind of weird was the garage door being up—most people draw them closed—and Freddie saying that's a blue car."

"Yeah, so?"

"Well, Freddie's car isn't blue. Neither is... was his wife's... and this is a pencil drawing." Mia could see he still didn't get it. She quickly took back her patient's drawing and handed her own painting to the detective.

"He did this?"

"No, this is a painting I did later. But look, the car is blue!'

"So? What's your point?"

Mia could feel the heat rising in her cheeks. This was a mistake. But she had to keep going now. "I know this may be hard to believe," she said, "but sometimes my drawings kind of come from... someone else." Mia could feel herself shaking. *He's not going to believe me.* She talked faster. "I mean, I don't plan or think about what I'm doing, and I'm surprised by the image I create."

His eyebrows were no longer raised and his gaze went to the window behind her. She knew she was losing him so she grabbed her painting and pointed to the tiny detail that she and Julie had noticed for the first time Saturday.

"What's that supposed to be?" he asked.

"I think it's an earring."

Bishop raised his eyes from the painting to look at her. Without a word he was saying what's your point.

"I... I didn't consciously draw it. But I... I thought it might be important. I mean you said to let you know about anything... no matter how small. So I thought maybe..."

"Sure. Well, I didn't see an earring, but I'll take another look. I doubt it would mean much anyway. Women lose earrings, right? Happens all the time. Could've been there a while." He closed his notepad without writing a word and turned to leave... then stopped abruptly by Mia's desk. She watched for a moment waiting.

"Detective?"

"Where did you get this?" he asked, whipping his head around to face her. His intense blue eyes seemed to bore into her and she stepped back.

"Wha-wha-what do you mean? I drew it."

Bishop stared at her in disbelief.

"Why," Mia asked. What's wrong?"

He didn't answer. Instead he asked, "Where? Where is this house?"

"I... I don't know. I just drew it."

"Whaddya mean, you just drew it? You must have seen it." He turned back to the drawing and touched it, ran his fingers over it, then narrowed his eyes and returned his gaze to Mia.

"It's one of those drawings I was telling you about," she said. "Why are you looking at me like that? What's wrong?"

"So you're telling me you've never seen this house before? You've never been there?"

"Yes," Mia said growing indignant, wondering if he was calling her a liar... accusing her of something. "What's wrong with you?" But then she was struck by a realization that gave her chills. This house was somehow familiar to him. She had to know why. "Detective, why are you so concerned about that house?"

Detective Bishop stared hard at the image, then at Mia, before lowering himself to the edge of her desk.

"Just call me Ron," he said softly. "I'm wondering why you say you've never seen it, but I'm staring at a picture of my family home."

CHAPTER TWENTY

R on barely noticed the chill running through him on such a warm spring day. He thought this Monday would be full of the usual tasks, following leads that went nowhere, poring over paperwork, returning calls to family members who wanted answers, and interviewing possible witnesses of a new weekend homicide.

There wasn't really much of a mystery to that one. Several people at a bar had witnessed the fight between the victim and the shooter, and the perp still had the gun in his possession when he was arrested. That and the money the killer had taken for the drugs he sold the guy then took back after he shot him. But still, Ron knew they had to follow the evidence and build a case so the D.A. could make it stick.

Back in his office he was finding it extremely difficult to focus on his latest case, or any of the others on his desk, when a familiar cold case kept creeping into his mind—the murder that had taken place in the house he'd just seen in Mia Reed's drawing. And the disappearance of his sister. It was a house he'd tried—with varying degrees of success—to put out of his mind since he was fifteen years old.

Shaking off the memory, Bishop picked up the Alessi file, opened his phone, and scrolled to the picture he'd taken of Mia's painting. Making it larger he stared at the detail she had pointed out. It was fairly hard to make out, but it was blue. A tiny jewel? A sapphire? Something clicked. Bishop sprang to his feet.

"I'm going down to evidence," he called to Barry, his fellow detective.

When he got to the evidence room, it didn't take long to find what he was looking for. There it was, just like he remembered.

The tiny sapphire and diamond earring had been on Claire Alessi's good side, not the side where her face had been battered and bruised.

Within thirty minutes of his discovery Bishop was at the Alessi house searching the front lawn for the missing piece of jewelry, but with no luck.

"Detective Bishop, what are you doing here?" Anthony asked.

Bishop hadn't heard the front door open and was surprised to see Freddie's brother standing in the doorway.

"Anthony, how's your brother doing?"

"He's coming along all right. But he saw you drive up, and when you didn't ring the bell, he asked me to find out what was going on."

"I'm looking for something."

"What's that? Maybe I can help," Anthony said leaning against the door frame.

"Yeah, maybe you can." Bishop stopped looking in the flower bed, brushed the dirt from his hands, and focused on the man standing above him. "Did anybody happen to find a piece of jewelry out here? An earring?"

"No, why?" Anthony answered quickly.

"Are you sure? Don't you want to check with your brother?"

"That's not necessary, Bishop. He hasn't been outside of the house since we brought him home from the hospital."

"Well, how do you know it wasn't lost prior to the break-in?" He noticed the other man's hesitation.

"Yeah, okay. I'll ask him," Anthony said. "But why would you be concerned about an earring lost before that? And why are you concerned about an earring anyway?"

"Just covering all my bases."

"Hold on," Anthony said disappearing back into the house without inviting Bishop to join him. When he returned moments later, he assured the detective Freddie didn't know anything about a missing earring. "What's this all about anyway?"

Bishop told him he was just following every lead, and watched Anthony for any response. Seeing nothing but a sneer, he headed back to his car but halfway there did an about-face. "Hold up," he called as Anthony was closing the door. "I need to talk to your brother."

"He's still pretty worn out from today's PT session, and that art therapist said she was going to stop by on her way home."

"Don't worry, this won't take long." Walking past big brother, Ron followed the sound of shouting straight to Freddie propped up on the couch and yelling into his phone. Seeing the detective, Freddie lowered his voice and abruptly ended his call.

"What is it, Detective? Have you found him? Did you find who killed my wife?" His voice got higher and louder with each question. Then he took a breath. "Is that why you're here?"

"No, Mr. Alessi, I mean Freddie." The young man had told him *Mr. Alessi* was his father and insisted he call him Freddie—not Fred, but Freddie. "I'm sorry. But we're following every lead. That's why I'm here." He took a seat on the edge of an easy chair that he figured from the floral pattern must have been chosen by the late Claire Alessi. The unmade hospital bed in the corner of the room and dirty dishes on the coffee table made him wonder just how much help his brother was. "I know Anthony already asked you about the earring," he said not missing the look exchanged by the brothers, "but I wondered... is it okay if I take a look around?" He had already searched the house for clues, but he hadn't been looking for an earring.

Permission given, he went up to the room he now knew to be the master bedroom and the place where Mrs. Alessi would keep her jewelry. With only a quick perusal of the room, he saw what he was looking for. He went directly to the brown walnut box and lifted the lid. He opened one drawer after another. When he got to the bottom drawer, he blew out his breath. No earring. He knew it had been a longshot, but sometimes longshots paid off. Not this time. Yet he was convinced the earring in Mia's picture was a match for the one in the evidence bag. The one they'd taken off their victim.

CHAPTER TWENTY-ONE

Mia parked by the curb and climbed the long uphill driveway. She recognized the blue car parked there as Anthony's but wasn't sure about the other car, a black Crown Victoria. Didn't matter though. She didn't want to park anybody in, or have to come back outside to move her car. Besides, she thought, it's a beautiful day, and the exercise wouldn't hurt. She enjoyed walking, and even with her portfolio she could manage this distance.

Halfway up the hill, she realized she could have saved herself the hike—and the perspiration—if she'd been just a few minutes later. The front door opened and a familiar figure walked out and stopped short when he saw her.

"Mia Reed?" the detective called down to her, shading his eyes. He didn't say anything else. Just stood waiting.

"Hello, Detective." Not sure what else to say, Mia moved to pass him, but he caught her arm before she could reach the door. She turned back to face him. *They really are the bluest eyes I've ever seen.* She waited knowing her face must be showing her puzzlement.

"I'm glad I ran into you," he said. "I... I... um... wanted to thank you for the tip."

It took a moment before Mia realized he might be talking about what she'd shown him in the drawing. "Oh, did it help? Really? Well, what was it?"

"It looks like it might have been an earring that belonged to Mrs. Alessi."

Mia tried to pump him for more information, but the detective didn't give her any direct answers and suddenly seemed to be in a hurry. "I have to get back to the precinct," he said, "but thanks, and if you think of anything else... call me. Please."

Mia watched as he drove away before knocking on the Alessi door, hoping Anthony would answer. He did. And he yanked the door open. But when he saw Mia, his demeanor softened and his eyes seemed to dance with amusement. Mia wasn't sure why that fired up her cheeks and made her ears burn, but she brushed past him asking where she would find her patient.

"Freddie's right through there," Anthony said pointing to the wide doorway to his right. "But before you go in, can I ask you something?"

"What is it?"

"I need to see you... tonight."

"That's not a question."

Anthony laughed at that. "Okay, may I see you tonight?" he asked dramatically... or sarcastically.

But Mia was quite sure he didn't expect and wouldn't take no for an answer. Besides, she couldn't think of any excuse not to agree. She also realized she didn't actually have any desire to say no.

"I suppose so, as long as we make it an early evening. Pick me up at 6:30?" After he agreed, he stole a quick kiss—for which Mia was completely unprepared—and took her to Freddie, then promptly disappeared.

Pushing Anthony from her mind to be fully present for her patient, Mia led Freddie through several minutes of deep breathing and guided imagery. She told him to imagine he was going down a golden staircase to a safe place, and as he reached the bottom step, she asked him to look around.

"Breathe in. Look around you... to your left... to your right, maybe above or below you. Now draw your peaceful place."

Freddie had appeared agitated and less than enthusiastic at the beginning of their session, but more peaceful now. He worked on his sketch using only the calming colors Mia had provided, and she observed the tension leaving his body. His shoulders dropped down from his ears and the deep lines in his forehead smoothed out.

In her limited experience, Mia had usually seen her patients produce images of the beach, a stream, or a sunset. One client had drawn a kitchen where she loved to bake. But this was the first time she'd seen someone's safe place look so barren. "Can you tell me about this place?"

"It's my office," Freddie said.

Mia realized she was looking at a representation of a desk and chair with a large window behind it. It didn't look like the most relaxing place to her, but that wasn't the point. For some reason, this must feel like a safe place to him.

"Freddie, can you tell me why this place makes you feel safe and at peace?"

Mia was shocked and dismayed when he violently crumpled and threw the picture down. She wasn't sure what she'd done wrong, and searched miserably for what to say next, wishing someone more experienced was there to tell her what to do.

But there was no one else. Feeling like a fraud, she looked at Freddie, hoping to find an answer, but he didn't return her gaze. He was staring somewhere behind her. She turned to face the doorway and saw nothing to agitate him. All she saw was his brother, Anthony.

"Do you mind?" she said to him. She really didn't need anyone interrupting their session at this moment.

"Sorry. I just thought you might want something to drink?"

Seriously? "No, Anthony. I appreciate it, but we're not quite finished here."

"Yes, I think we are," Freddie said. He had lain back against the big pillow on the end of the couch and thrown his arm over his forehead. "I've had enough for today. I'm tired."

Mia felt even more defeated. She'd agitated her patient instead of making him feel peaceful and relaxed. Flushed and frustrated, she gathered everything back into her portfolio and stood to leave. "I'm sorry, Freddie," she said. "Maybe next time we'll have more success."

"Yeah, maybe," Freddie said with a tone that had moved from angry to sullen.

Anxious to escape, Mia hurried toward the door, but just as she reached it, Anthony called to her. "I'll see you later."

CHAPTER TWENTY-TWO

Anthony was as good as his word. He did see Mia later... much later.

Mia remembered telling him to pick her up at 6:30. But 6:30 came and went. By 7:10 she was miffed and certain she'd been stood up. She was tired of pacing back and forth in her tiny apartment and, with one last look out the window, kicked off her flats and laced on her walking shoes.

Simeon, ever vigilant, jumped down from his perch high atop his tower, and meowed his concern. "Yes Simmie, I'm going for a walk, and I know I didn't brush you yet," Mia said. "Be patient." Not bothering to change out of her casual outfit into her usual walking clothes, she was ready to walk off her frustration before dark.

Mia yanked open the front door and came face to face with her date. She made an obvious show of checking the time on her phone then raised her chin in defiance. Though typically easy-going, she didn't like being made the fool.

"Going somewhere?" Anthony asked grinning. Then his smile faded. "I didn't know you had a cat," he stated flatly.

"Well, I do. Do you have a problem with cats?" Mia asked defensively.

"I just don't see the point."

"I do, and yes," Mia said. "I decided you must not be coming so I was going for a walk." She noticed the quick lashing back and forth of Simeon's tail and scooped him up before he could start any trouble or wander out into the hall.

"Well, I'm here now, so shall we go grab a bite?" He was still smiling. No apology. No explanation.

Mia closed her mouth and spun back into the apartment, unsure what to say. When she turned to face him again, he still hadn't wiped the grin off his face. She wanted to scream at him, but she was speechless. Besides, people in her family didn't scream. Thinking about what her mom would say to do instead, Mia took a deep breath, and gave him what she was sure was an icy glare.

"What's wrong, darlin'? You look like you could skin a rat."

Yes, and you're the rat I could skin.

But then Anthony lifted her chin and kissed her gently, briefly, their lips merely grazing each other, and said, "I'm sorry I kept you waiting."

Pulling her to him, he kissed her, deeply this time, taking her breath away. She felt him moving forward so she was forced to step back. One step, then two, three... *Is he trying to get to my bedroom?* When he finally released her, Mia couldn't decide whether to scold him or lean in for more. But if he intended what she feared he might, she would have to stop him.

Fortunately, her roommate burst in, disrupting the moment. "Oh, hello there," Morgan said. "Sorry. Am I interrupting something?"

Simeon, tail still wagging, added his own meow of disapproval.

"No," Mia said quickly. "We were just leaving."

Morgan laughed. "Okay, if you say so."

Mia felt her embarrassment in her cheeks and was irritated knowing her face would tell all. She was even more annoyed by the amusement she saw in Anthony's eyes She grabbed her jacket and Anthony's hand, stuck her tongue out at laughing Morgan on the way past, and didn't realize until they were driving away that she was still wearing her sneakers.

As it turned out, it didn't matter what was on her feet. "Where are we going?" Mia asked as Anthony drove away from the city.

"It's a surprise."

Not being a big fan of surprises, Mia wondered why men seemed to feel the need to take charge and surprise them instead of simply saying what was on their mind. And the uncertainty of where she was being taken made her think of another time when she had been driven to a cabin in the woods and kept there against her will. Shaking off the memory of her kidnapping when she had been only fourteen, Mia did her best to stay in the present. After all, the man driving was not a stranger, and she had no reason to be afraid.

When Anthony pulled into the parking garage of a large building and took her into the elevator, she asked, "Is there a restaurant in this building?"

"Yes," he said with a mischievous grin. "Chez Alessi."

Mia cautiously followed him off the elevator and into his apartment. Nervous as a schoolgirl, she trailed him through the entryway, where she could see past the open kitchen into the dining and living areas. The table—set for two, with a bottle of Riesling in an ice bucket—was lovely. But there was no food. There was no smell of food cooking either.

Without a word, Anthony went to the table, uncorked the wine, and generously filled two glasses and brought one to her. "A toast to the pretty and patient Ms. Reed."

The Riesling was delicious, but Mia felt—and heard—her stomach growling. She was used to eating anytime between five-thirty and seven o'clock, but it was nearly eight. Now, adding to her earlier embarrassment, Anthony laughed at her audible rumbling. "It sounds like you need to be fed, young lady."

Young lady? Just because she was nearly ten years younger didn't make her a child. Besides, he hadn't kissed her like he thought anything of the kind.

Putting her indignation aside in favor of dealing with her hunger, she looked around. "Your place is really nice, and this is a delicious wine. But, yes, I am hungry. You were kind of late picking me up, remember?"

"Have no fear. The food should be here any time now," Anthony said. And as if on cue, there was a knock on the door.

When he opened it Mia didn't need to ask what they were having. The wonderful aroma of Chinese food floated from the big brown bag straight to her salivary glands. In no time, Anthony was pulling white boxes out of the bag.

"I hope you like Chinese," he said.

Mia loved Chinese food and was actually pleased with what he'd chosen, but thought it might have been nice to ask first. It was becoming more and more obvious, Anthony liked to be the decision maker.

Between bites of the spare ribs she was enjoying from their pu pu platter, Mia asked, "So how was your brother after I left?"

The line between Anthony's brows deepened. "Okay, I think. He's been having a lot of angry blowouts ever since he came home. Can't blame him, I guess. After all he's been through. But then he's always had a nasty temper."

"I'm worried about him."

"Well yeah. Of course, I am too." Anthony put his fork down and sipped his wine. "But do we have to talk about my little brother tonight? I've been spending most of my time dealing with his moods."

He put his glass down so hard its recently filled contents spilled over. Mia watched him take a deep breath, regaining his composure as he mopped it up with his napkin. It seemed Freddie wasn't the only Alessi with a short fuse.

A moment later, he had also repaired his face, putting the smile back where it had been moments before she mentioned Freddie. "So tell me, Mia, what do you do with your time when you're not working at the hospital or making house calls?"

"I paint."

Chapter Twenty-three

It wasn't long before Mia read boredom on Anthony's face. He was obviously losing interest in hearing about her love of drawing, painting and the arts, so Mia searched for another subject. She asked him about his own interests which seemed limited to his business and his little brother.

"Tell me, have you and Freddie always been this close?"

"Always?" Anthony looked at the ceiling. "I guess it kind of feels that way. At least since the time he took a bad fall when he was about five years old." He paused and chuckled. "We were just playing, you know, wrestling on the floor—and he was laughing—but then he hit his head on the coffee table. It was pretty bad. The folks said he had a concussion, and I guess they blamed me because I was older." He pushed back in his chair and laughed again. "After that, it seemed like anytime he hurt himself—and he was a klutz—they figured it must be my fault. Said I should look out for him."

Mia had noticed the change in his expression and the sound of his humorless laugh and wished she hadn't asked. "That must have been hard," she said in an effort to help. "But I know Freddie really looks up to you."

Anthony tilted his head and squinted his eyes. "So here we are talking about little brother again. I'm beginning to think you're more interested in him than me."

Mia tried to object, but his expression morphed again. She saw the same beguiling look that had drawn her in earlier. The one that made her forget his late arrival and brash behavior.

They had been sitting at the table so long Mia's bottom was getting tired in spite of the padding on the chair, so when Anthony suggested moving to the living room, she was happy to oblige.

The white leather sofa was comfortable, but not nearly as comfortable as the beast. Still, Mia admired Anthony's taste in decorating. This room looked like something out of a magazine. It didn't have the warm, homey feel of her parents' or grandparents' places, or even her own little apartment, though. Something was lacking. She found herself searching for something personal—anything that said Anthony—but she didn't find it.

Anthony filled her wine glass for the third time before settling next to her, and though she rarely had more than one or two glasses, she accepted and enjoyed the warmth it gave her. When Anthony slid closer and took her hand and raised it to his lips, her heart beat faster. She wondered if he could hear it as it pounded in her ears.

Taking the glass from her hand and putting it on the coaster behind her, Anthony slowly moved so close she couldn't breathe. Then his arms wrapped around her, and he kissed her until her entire body burned with desire. She was nearly lost in the hunger and knew she had to escape.

"Stop," she said after pulling away.

"Why?" he murmured, pulling her in again. His lips sought hers once more and his hands wandered dangerously.

With herculean effort Mia pushed him back and jumped to her feet. There was a moment of absolute quiet. Even the soft mood music he'd had playing from somewhere in the apartment paused in that moment.

As Mia stood lightheaded, swaying slightly with her back to Anthony, she grappled with what to do next. She was shocked when the silence was broken.

"What's your problem?" Anthony's tone was not a gentle question. It was a snarky accusation.

He covered the distance between them before she could react, grasped her shoulders and spun her around. The kiss he now forced on her did not summon those same passionate responses. Her heart beat faster, but with fear rather than fervor, and she burned with anger not lust.

"Stop it, Anthony!" she managed to declare, breaking free.

Mia knew she'd be no match for him if he persisted, but in an instant his determination vanished, and his face hardened. He bolted across the room to the kitchen, snatched his phone from the counter where he'd left it during dinner, and quickly thumbed the keys.

What is he doing? Mia couldn't move. Didn't know what to do. She thought of running for the door but her feet were glued to the floor. Anthony casually slipped the phone back into his pocket and turned to face her, leaning casually against the bar.

"I ordered you an Uber. Satisfied? Should be here in eight minutes. Why don't you go wait in the lobby?" Without another word, he moved past her, causing her to flinch as his shoulder brushed hers. He stopped by her side and sneered, "Don't worry, little girl. I'm not in the habit of having to force a woman into my bed."

"I'm sorry," Mia whispered to his back as he slammed his bedroom door. She picked up her bag and made her way to the door, looking back once, thinking she heard him open it. But he wasn't there. She heard nothing but a quiet click of the latch catching.

She managed to hold it together on the ride back, and was surprised when the Uber driver told her to put her money away—it was already taken care of—and prayed Morgan would already be in bed.

Mia slid the key in the lock as quietly as she could and let out her breath when she saw the only light was the one left on over the stove. It was enough to make her way to the bedroom and silently close the door behind her. Dropping her bag on the floor she flopped down on her bed and let the tears finally roll down her cheeks.

After allowing herself several minutes to let out all the pent up hurt and frustration of the night, Mia wandered back out to the kitchen, opened the refrigerator door, and searched for something to ease the gnawing in her stomach. Finding nothing that didn't require more energy to prepare than she had to spare, she considered a peanut butter sandwich. She removed the lid and the smell of the peanut butter took her back to her time locked in a cage when she had been given that food to survive. Finally settling on a bagel and cream cheese, she returned to her room, wiped away new tears, and began brushing Simeon. The repetitive motion and Simmie's soft purrs brought calm as the moments passed.

When she was satisfied the brushing time was over—thanks to Simeon letting her know he'd had enough—she reached for her journal. Writing her thoughts and feelings she'd discovered was the next best thing to talking to Julie, and though it wasn't much after ten, she knew her sister might already be sleeping. Julie always said she needed her eight to ten hours sleep and her two coffees in the morning before she could have a productive day. Mia, on the other hand, rarely slept for more than seven hours, and she knew the sandman wasn't going to be visiting her any time soon.

Mia let her pen say all the things she knew she'd been holding in... and some she hadn't known...

She wrote until her fingers ached. She wrote until she was done. And when she reread the words on the page, she searched for that welcomed sense of relief. It didn't come. Defeated, she had to push herself to go through her nightly ritual, and finally with her pajamas donned, she crawled into bed. Sleep would come soon. She could skip her usual bedtime reading but not her prayers. Mia turned off the light and spoke to God. She thanked Him for her many blessings, especially her family, and then asked for His help.

I don't know what I'm doing wrong, Lord. I know I made him mad tonight. Maybe if he knew me better. Was I wrong not to tell him about my faith? Would he understand then? Her mind drifted from her prayers and she thought something was off. Then, as she was slipping into sleep, she thought, *Maybe if I'd told him I'm a virgin...*

Chapter Twenty-four

R on Bishop watched as Freddie examined the picture. He was glad to have some time alone with the younger Alessi brother. Anthony was lurking around somewhere in the house, but with a few persuasive hints, Ron had managed to at least get him out of the room.

"I couldn't swear to it, but yeah, that looks like one of her earrings. I gave them to her on our first wedding anniversary," Freddie said without looking up from the photo Ron had given him. "We were supposed to go back to Paris this summer for our f-fifth..." Freddie's voice cracked on the final word and Ron saw him swallow hard.

"I'm sorry, Freddie. I know how difficult this must be for you."

"Do you?" Freddie snapped, jutting out his chin. "Was your wife murdered?"

Ron took a deep breath. "No, I'm truly sorry."

He hadn't lost a wife—he'd never even had a wife—but he did know how it felt to have someone you love murdered. And he'd never forget it. But he had no need to defend himself. Besides, that wouldn't help Freddie, and he'd learned anger was a huge part of the grieving process. He couldn't fault the man for his reaction. He reached to take the picture back and slid it into the blue folder.

"Have you been able to recall anything more about how you wound up at the bottom of the steps? Any memory of a face? Anything?"

"No. I mean nothing about who did this. Don't you think I would've called you if I had?"

"Sure, I guess," Ron said, "but is there something else you do remember?"

"Well yeah, but it's not anything important. Not gonna help."

"How 'bout you let me be the judge of that. You never know," Ron said, pen poised to take down any detail.

"Okay, well, I didn't remember coming back from the office until yesterday. Now I do. And I know why. I forgot something I really needed for a client meeting that afternoon. I had tried to call Claire to bring it to me, since she had the day off, but she didn't answer her phone. I remember getting aggravated. I mean, like I've told her before, what's the point of having a cell phone if you're not going to answer it? So anyhow, I had to come home to get it." Freddie pulled his hand through his hair and shook his head. He looked up at Ron. "And I must've walked in on something..." he said just as Anthony intruded

"Oh, Detective. You're still here. I don't mean to interrupt, but Freddie's therapist should be here soon, so..." Ron was sure he did indeed mean to interrupt, and he didn't need to be hit with a brick to know he was being asked to leave. But then again, hearing Mia Reed would be there soon made him more inclined to linger.

"Don't worry, Anthony. We're about finished here." Ron stood and moved toward the door, then turned back to face big brother. "Before I go, have you thought of anything else? Anything at all from when you found your brother?" Anthony denied remembering anything he hadn't already shared. "Okay then. But call me if you do," Ron said reaching in his pocket and handing over his card.

"Okay, sure. I'll put this with the other ones you've given me." Anthony smirked.

Ron said he'd see himself out and assured Freddie he'd keep him posted on any new developments in the case. He heard the "*hmpf*" as he exited the room—not sure which brother—but chose to ignore it and be on his way.

After dragging his feet to get to his vehicle, he sat behind the wheel checking messages on his phone and frequently glancing in his rearview mirror. Just as he was about to give up, he saw the car he'd been watching and waiting for. Her red Honda Civic pulled into the driveway behind Anthony's car, and Ron got out and walked around to meet the driver. She was pulling her portfolio out of the back when he came up behind her.

"Can I help you with that?" Ron asked. Mia jumped and let out a little squeal. "Whoa, I didn't mean to startle you..." They both had to laugh, and Ron was charmed by her childlike giggle and the dimple that appeared each time she smiled.

"Thanks, but I've got this. I'm used to lugging it around."

"Wait," Ron said as she reached the sidewalk leading to the front door of the Alessi home. When she spun back to face him, he noticed how the sun highlighted her hair with flecks of gold. He searched wildly for something to say, then recalled the drawing. "I, um, I wondered if I could maybe stop by the hospital later and take another look at that drawing you showed me last week."

"The one with that earring or whatever it was?"

"No, the other one. The house that looked like my family home. You described it as one of your *special* drawings."

Mia tilted her head ever so slightly, gave him a quizzical look, then agreed. She said she'd be back by lunchtime. "How about around one o'clock?"

"It's a date," he said reaching out to shake her hand and not wanting to let it go.

Ron hopped back in and started his car, then watched as Anthony opened the door for Mia. And he didn't miss the look the other man shot at him before closing the door behind her.

Driving back to the precinct, Ron mulled over the facts of the Claire Alessi case—the unanswered questions—Anthony's hovering behavior, Freddie's anger, and the little bit of memory Freddie had gotten back. Maybe he'd get more. The doctor had said it was possible, just no guarantee.

But the detective's mind kept skipping back to the girl with a dimple and gold flecks in her hair.

CHAPTER TWENTY-FIVE

$\mathcal{M}$ia whisked past Anthony straight into the living room where she'd worked with Freddie the previous Monday, but the room was empty. Several pillows were shoved to one end of the sofa, and the raspberry floral afghan had been tossed across the back, yet there was no sign of her patient. She spun around only to see his big brother leaning in the doorway looking quite amused.

"He's in the bathroom," Anthony said.

Mia waited for him to say more, but he stood there simply smiling—or was it a smirk—without saying another word.

When he finally broke the silence, Mia's mouth dropped open. "Let's do dinner tonight." No apology for the way he'd treated her at his apartment; no explanation for why he hadn't called since. Nothing.

Before she could even begin to sputter out her indignation, she was interrupted by the sound of Freddie's crutches.

Anthony must have heard them too and turned to meet him. "Doing all right there, little brother?"

Freddie grumbled something under his breath, then seeing Mia, stopped. "Is it that time already?" he asked. He lowered himself onto the couch, dropped his crutches on the floor and emitted a huge sigh. "Gimme a minute," he said catching his breath.

Mia was happy to give him all the time he needed to get situated so she could use that same time to compose herself. Intending to give Anthony a look that would tell him exactly what she thought of his inappropriate proposal, she snapped her head back in his direction. But he didn't get to see the icy glare she'd prepared for him. He had quietly vanished once again. *He's like a ghost.*

With great effort, Mia put her full attention on her patient for the next forty-five minutes, but she struggled to ignore the itchy tingling that had started in her right hand when Ron Bishop shook it. She recognized the feeling and knew she would have to answer its call—and the sooner, the better.

Freddie made minimal effort with his therapy and showed more desire to turn off than tune in to his thoughts and emotions that day. Monosyllabic responses to open-ended questions led nowhere, and Mia packed up her supplies, disappointed in herself for being unable to draw him out more.

"Is there anything else I can do for you before I leave, Freddie?" she asked grabbing the handle of her portfolio. "Can I get you anything?"

"No, Anthony's still here—seems like he's afraid to leave me alone—and I'm getting around better the last few days. I wish everyone would leave, especially him, and stop asking if I remember anything. Anyway, everything I need is down here, so..." He looked toward the door, and Mia wondered if he was looking for his brother or possibly thinking about the stairs, and what had happened, or what lay beyond.

"You're sure you're okay then?" she asked hoping for a late epiphany, while also hoping to quickly return to the hospital to scratch the itch nagging at her fingertips.

Freddie repeated that he had all he needed and waved her away, so portfolio in hand, Mia headed for the front door, but not without scanning the entryway and portals to other parts of the house for any sign of Anthony.

Back in her Civic, she was both relieved and disappointed. *"Let's do dinner tonight,"* Anthony had said before disappearing. Like nothing strange had happened the week before. Like he hadn't sent her home in an Uber when he didn't get his way. *He's got a lot of nerve.* And he hadn't waited around for a response. He was certainly an enigma taking up way too much space and time in her brain on the drive back to the hospital. Shaking her head,

Mia decided he was not a puzzle she had time to try to figure out now.

With only fleeting greetings to coworkers, Mia hastened to the quiet of her office—happy her mentor worked with patients in a nearby nursing home on Monday afternoons—and took up her watercolor pencils which began flying across the special heavy paper. She worked furiously, and quickly completed the drawing without conscious thought. When it was done, she looked at the face of a lovely, blonde-haired, blue-eyed young woman she'd never seen before. Yet there was something so familiar about the eyes. She'd seen those piercing blue eyes before.

"Hello?" Totally engrossed in what she'd been drawing, Mia hadn't heard him come in.

"Oh, Detective, yes. Come in, please," she said putting her work aside. "You said you wanted another look at the house." Mia crossed the room to retrieve the "spirit inspired" picture he was interested in.

As she leafed through the drawings, Ron asked, "How was your patient today?"

"You saw him. What did you think? How was his mood when you were there?"

"Pretty sullen, but at least he got back a little memory of the day he was assaulted."

"Really?" Mia's brow shot up, stunned Freddie hadn't mentioned it to her. "Does he know who's responsible? Who killed his wife?"

"No. Nothing like that. But at least he now remembers why he returned home from his office. So, I'm guessing he could remember more."

Mia handed him the picture he'd come to see and returned to her seat while he studied it.

She thought the look on his face spoke of longing. "What is it, Detective?"

"Ron, please," he said. Then settling into the chair across from her, he said, "Mia, tell me more about this gift you say you have. How do you think you've come to draw my house? And why?"

Mia tried to explain, though she doubted he would understand or believe. Yet maybe... She told him about the cabin she'd drawn so many years ago—a cabin she'd never seen or been to—before being kidnapped and how someone recognized that very cabin. She briefly explained the circumstances of how they found and rescued her because of that drawing and what she knew was the help of God. Though it sounded incredible, she knew it was true. And when she looked in his eyes something said he might believe her. *Those eyes...*

Mia hesitated only briefly before saying, "I have another picture I'd like to show you." She slowly revealed the image of the young woman and watched Ron's jaw drop. He stared with incredulity, and Mia saw the tears start to fill his eyes before he jumped up and turned away. When he spun back, he looked angry.

"Who is she?" he demanded. His normally husky voice became a growl. "Tell me!"

"I, I don't know who she is. I thought you might... I, I've never seen her before."

"Why would you think I might know?" The words were a challenge. One she hesitated to take. *But I've come this far.*

"I don't know, exactly, but the eyes." Mia tried to hide her embarrassment, certain she was making a fool of herself, but forced the rest of her explanation out. "They look like your eyes." His head jerked up, and those same eyes locked with hers. But he said nothing. "Ron, you know her, don't you?" Mia said softly. "Who is she?"

"Her name," he swallowed hard, cleared his throat, and started again. "Her name is Robin. And the last time I saw her she was much younger." It was almost a whisper. He stared at the image before him, then slowly moved his tear-filled eyes up to meet hers. "She's my twin sister, Robin."

CHAPTER TWENTY-SIX

Dumbfounded, Ron couldn't take his eyes off the image of his sister. Not a fifteen-year-old girl, but a woman. She would be turning thirty on their birthday, June 19th. But was it possible after all these years? Could she really be alive somewhere? And if so, where was she? Where had she been for the nearly fifteen years she'd been missing?

His eyes traveled from the picture of Robin to the face of the artist and back again. *How?* She said something. What had she said? "I'm sorry... what?"

"I said, are you and your sister close? Does she live nearby?" Mia asked.

Of course, Mia doesn't know. "No. I mean yes, we were close, but no, she doesn't live around here. At least... I don't think so." The words tumbled out. "I mean I haven't seen her since we were fifteen." He remembered exactly when he'd last seen Robin. It was July 19th—just one month after their birthday—and they'd sat around the dinner table just like any other day. Robin had been bubbling over about their upcoming family trip to Disney, a birthday gift about which she was terribly excited. Ron was ashamed of what he'd been thinking.

All he had wanted to do was stay home and hang with his buddies. They were starting up a band and wanted him to be lead singer, but the real draw was the keyboard player, Janie Karns. Having to spend nearly ten days with his parents and sister wouldn't be so bad, but he'd much rather be hanging out with Janie. That night at dinner he had been trying to figure out how to get out of spending time with his boring family instead of her.

In the aftermath of the night he lost them all, Ron remembered the guilt he'd carried.

"Ron, are you okay?" Mia's voice brought him back to the present. And it brought him back to all his questions. So many unanswered questions.

Yet all he could think to ask was, "Why did you draw this?"

"I had no choice."

Ron didn't understand. Part of him wanted to believe her, but then there was the suspicious part of his cop brain that wondered what kind of game she was playing.

"I know how strange this must seem to you," she said. "It took me a long time to accept and get used to, but I finally realized it's a special kind of gift, and when it happens—this urge to draw something I don't understand—I simply have to do it."

Ron got up. Sat back down. Looked into the eyes of Mia Reed and somehow knew she was telling the truth. "I don't get it. I really don't... but I want to." He rubbed the perspiration from his palms onto his pants. He saw the puzzled, almost pained expression on Mia's face. "Listen, you don't understand. Robin disappeared fifteen years ago," Ron said.

Mia's jaw dropped, and the color drained from her face.

"I know you have patients to see," he added having seen her check the time, "but I need to ask you more about this. Could we maybe get together later and talk? I have so many questions, and..."

Ron had learned to read people, usually suspects, pretty well, and the indecision he saw on Mia's face made his heart drop.

"I, um, I'm sorry. I can't today. I sort of already have a commitment tonight."

"Yeah, okay." He slowly got to his feet still searching for some way to change her mind. He needed answers... and he didn't want to beg, but he would if it came to that.

"But Ron, maybe tomorrow?" she added.

His heart jumped at that. When they'd set a time and place to meet, he thanked her and made to leave but turned back before reaching the door.

"One more thing," he said. "The picture. Would you mind if I took it with me?"

"Of course, it's yours," she said immediately. "But wait." She grabbed her phone and took a shot of the watercolor. "I like to keep a record of my work."

Ron's hand touched hers when he accepted the painting, and he wanted to stay, to hold that hand. He hadn't felt this kind of attraction to a woman in a very long time.

Shake it off, man! You don't know anything about her. What if this was some kind of crazy scam?

CHAPTER TWENTY-SEVEN

Mia did her best to stay focused on each of her patients for the rest of the day, but it wasn't easy. As she was cleaning up the art room after her final group of five children from the pediatric wing, all the questions came tumbling in on her. Many were about her most recent watercolor, the pretty blonde, but the biggest question of all had nothing to do with that or with Ron. *Why did I say I had a commitment tonight?*

But she knew why. She certainly hadn't told Anthony she'd see him. He hadn't even waited for an answer. *"Let's do dinner,"* he had said. That wasn't a question. Mia put the final bin back on the shelf and straightened it. Her action made her think of Amber putting everything in its exact place. Mia wasn't quite that particular, but she didn't want Pat, her mentor, unable to find something because the newbie put it on the wrong shelf.

Satisfied with her cleanup, Mia raced back to her office, did a quick check of the next day's schedule—Tuesdays were the easiest as a rule—and seeing tomorrow would be no different headed out.

She gave Morgan a quick wave as she passed the nurses' station and heard her roommate call, "See you at home." Probably true. She hadn't heard from Anthony since his disappearance that morning, and she hadn't agreed to have dinner with him either. So he surely wouldn't show up on her doorstep. Yet she'd kept the evening open just in case. *What's wrong with me,* she wondered on the drive home.

But when she arrived, she strode straight to the bedroom and pulled out her scoop-necked emerald tunic top with decorative scrolling and tiny sequin details. After changing into that and her best black slacks, she assessed the result in the full-length mirror hanging on the back of her door. Something was missing. She scurried back to her jewelry box and lifted out her silver-plated cross with the clear and green cubic zirconia, a gift from her grandmother's best friend, the woman she called Aunt Bonnie. A pair of tiny sapphire earrings—a gift she'd purchased for herself last summer—caught her eye. She touched them, realizing how similar they were to the one she'd unwittingly put in the painting of the Alessi house. Shaking off the memory, she put them back and selected tiny crystal earrings that worked better with her cross. She did another check and smiled at the result.

While looking at her reflection, Mia's smile slowly faded. *What am I doing?* She toyed with the idea of changing again, only this time into her more comfortable workout clothes. But hearing movement in the hall, she hesitated.

Morgan found Mia standing in her bedroom doorway with a look of disappointment sprawled across her face. "Wow, you sure look glad to see me," she joked. "Are you expecting Prince Charming?"

"No. I don't know."

"What's that supposed to mean? You surely didn't get that dolled up for me," Morgan said dropping her keys in the bowl by the door. "So, what's up?"

Mia told her roommate about the brief exchange—if you could even call it that—between her and Anthony earlier in the day and watched the crease between Morgan's brows deepen.

"I can't believe you'd even consider going out with him after the way he's treated you. Are you really going to let him get away with that?"

"I'm sure he didn't mean anything by it."

"Mia, come on..."

"But you haven't seen the other side of him. I mean, he can really be so sweet, and he makes me feel..." Mia searched for the words but couldn't find them. There weren't words for the way she felt when he kissed her. And she was sure she must have overreacted the last time they were together.

"I think that's just hormones or pheromones or something—"

"Besides, I don't think he's coming," Mia interrupted.

A knock on the door was evidence she was incorrect, and when she hesitated, Morgan was quick to ask, "Do you want me to get rid of him?"

"No!" Mia opened the door while Morgan stood, hands on hips, right behind her. "Let me get my bag," Mia said dashing back to her bedroom to grab it. When she returned seconds later, Anthony stood staring at Morgan, eyebrows raised.

Then Morgan unexpectedly gave Mia a hug and whispered, "Call if you need me."

Once in the car, Mia realized Anthony hadn't said a word since showing up. And he didn't seem at all surprised that she was dressed and ready to go with him. The heat rising in her now had nothing to do with the passion he stirred with his kisses. This heat rose out of anger. Giving him a sidelong glance and seeing the smug look on his face fueled the fire that had begun to burn in her gut.

"Anthony," she said evenly, "I've changed my mind. I think you should take me home."

"What? Why? What's wrong, kid?"

"First of all, I'm not a kid, and second, well, this is a mistake."

He didn't respond, nor did he make any attempt to turn the car around.

"I'm serious, Anthony." She studied his face for any sign of emotion, but his demeanor was flat, as was his voice when he finally replied.

"Why is this a mistake?" Then before she could reply, his face transformed. There was the charming smile and eyes that beckoned her. Even his voice changed when he went on. "Mia, love, I'm sorry if I hurt your feelings. Let me make it up to you. Please," he said looking at her and taking his eyes off the road too long.

"Be careful," Mia said as the car swerved back into his lane. As usual he was driving faster than she thought safe. He was still driving away from the city and gaining speed.

"Yeah, okay, but are we good?" When he looked her way again, she quickly agreed then felt the car slow down as his smile grew broader. "Good girl," he said patting her leg and taking her hand in his.

The rest of the ride to their destination was done in silence, and somehow the warmth of his hand softened her anger. She relaxed more knowing he wasn't heading in the direction of his apartment.

When he finally stopped the car, they were at the same scenic overlook where he'd brought her before. Her stomach was rumbling, and she had no intention of giving in to him if he was planning on pushing her further than she was ready to go.

"Have you already eaten? Because I haven't and—"

Anthony shut her up by putting his mouth on hers. Though she wanted to resist, Mia felt herself melting into him.

Chapter Twenty-eight

When Anthony finally released his hold on her, Mia pulled back and turned toward the window. Her mind was racing, and though she was drawn to him like nails to a magnet, her every instinct said run. "Anthony, what do you want from me?"

"I don't know what you mean. I like you... I want to spend time with you, that's all."

"Well, I'm sorry, but I don't think this is a good idea. I... I really think you should take me home."

"I thought you were hungry," he said. "Let's go get something to eat then."

"No! I said I want to go home." She turned to him and gave him the look she had prepared for him earlier in the day. This time there was no doubt he saw it, nor was there any doubt he didn't like it. Slamming the car in gear, he spun out of the parking area and onto the roadway without even looking for oncoming traffic. Mia held her breath and prayed he was taking her home and that they would get back in one piece.

Relief swept over her when he let his foot off the accelerator and slowed to a safer speed. With a glance his way, Mia saw his expression had softened, and the icy silence slowly appeared to thaw.

They hadn't gone more than a mile when a sudden *thump, thump, thump,* followed by a flapping noise was joined by a string of obscenities Mia found repugnant. Anthony's face had turned so red with rage that Mia was afraid to speak—or even breathe.

As soon as he found a safe spot, Anthony pulled off the road, and without another word, got out of the car to change the tire. Mia considered getting out to help, yet wanted to keep her distance. She thought of all the reasons he shouldn't expect her to pitch in, then she thought of all her parents had taught her about kindness.

Picturing the devil on one shoulder and an angel on the other, Mia laughed at herself and got out of the Tesla. She found Anthony, hands on his hips staring at what was left of the driver's side front tire. "Wow, that's really flat," she said, realizing how stupid it sounded as soon as the words were out of her mouth.

"Ya think?" Anthony said.

"Do you have a spare?"

"Of course," he answered, voice dripping with condescension. Anthony went to the trunk with Mia following at a safe distance.

He hauled the spare and a tire jack to the front of the car and asked Mia to grab the lug wrench. She was surprised at how dirty and muddy the trunk was for a man who kept himself, his apartment, and even the interior of his vehicle immaculate. But there was something else. Something she couldn't quite put her finger on...

It didn't take long for Anthony to make the change, lower the vehicle off of the jack, and tighten the lug nuts on the spare. He threw everything back in the trunk. With only a few more expletives he brushed the dirt from his clothes and jumped back into the driver's seat.

Mia was left standing by the front of the car staring in at him. without so much as a thanks.

She stomped around to her side. He hadn't even bothered to thank her. She got in and slammed the car door. Mia's deliberate show of annoyance brought no more than a sidelong glance of derision from Anthony. *He really is a jerk.*

"So how did Freddie's session go today?" Anthony asked pulling back onto the road.

Where did that come from? Mia was taken by surprise and more than a little maddened by the question. "That's not really for me to say. Why don't you ask him yourself?"

Anthony threw her a puzzled look that quickly altered into one of exasperation. "I asked *you*! What's your problem?" When Mia didn't respond he finally said, "Look, I'm worried about my little brother, all right? I just want to know if he remembered anything more about that day. That damn detective was bugging him this morning, and he's been in kind of a weird mood since."

Mia contemplated what he said and did recall Freddie being in a less than receptive mood when she'd tried to work with him. But he was injured, he couldn't remember what happened the day he was assaulted, and his wife was gone forever. Why wouldn't he be moody or depressed? "I'm sorry, Anthony, but I really can't help you. And I don't think you should blame Ron. He's just doing his job."

"Ron? It's Ron now?"

Mia didn't like the scornful look on Anthony's face and sighed with a mix of disappointment and relief as they pulled up in front of her apartment building. She wasn't sure what to say, so she said nothing, got out of the car, and watched the blue Tesla race away.

There was no goodbye from either of them, but Mia knew all the same. It was over.

Back in the apartment, she went straight for the fridge. The gnawing in her stomach demanded to be dealt with immediately.

"Well, that was quick," Morgan called over the back of the couch where she sat curled up eating a bowl of butter pecan ice cream. "What happened?"

"Nothing. He's a jerk, and I'm hungry." Mia pulled out the leftover meatloaf she'd made for their Sunday dinner, threw a couple pieces in the microwave, and sliced up an apple to share with Simeon who was patiently watching and waiting.

"So Prince Charming is more of a frog, huh?"

"Yeah, more like a Jekyll and Hyde, and I think I deserve better."

"Yeah, you do. Come join me. There's nothing worth watching on TV tonight so I'm checking Netflix. Any preference?"

As distracted as she was, Mia had no real interest in watching a movie. "Not really," she replied.

"Wanna talk about it?" Morgan asked.

"Not really." Mia didn't know how she felt and didn't think talking about it would bring any clarity. Her roommate was great about not pushing when Mia was like this. She always gave her space. So when she'd finished wolfing down her meager supper, she was delighted to find a new gallon of fudge ripple, then dished out a generous helping and retreated to her room... but not before Morgan jumped up and wrapped her in a warm hug.

"Don't forget. I'm here for you," Morgan said, and Simmie added one of his rare meows to let her knew he was too.

Mia returned the embrace, thanked her roommate, and scooped Simmie into her arms, thanking God for sending her such special friends.

Hunger satisfied, Mia checked the time and decided it was still early enough. She pulled her phone out and hit her favorites. Seconds later she was looking at her closest friend in the world... someone always there with a ready ear and a virtual shoulder to cry on when needed.

"Hey, what's up?" Julie was already in her oversized nightshirt. "Is something wrong?"

"No, not really. You look like you're headed to bed already."

"No, not yet," Julie said. "I've got a deadline to meet and need to proof this article one more time before I send it in." After assuring Mia she had time to talk, Julie asked again, "So come on, sis, what's going on? It's Monday. Not your usual time to call."

It didn't take long before Mia had unloaded the whole Anthony saga on her sister, and the very telling of it all somehow took away some of the sting. Julie, as was her way, didn't tell Mia what to do, but intuitively asked all the right questions to lead Mia to the conclusion she already knew. She was done with the older Alessi brother.

"By next Monday, I think Freddie will be able to come in for his appointment. And even if he's not, and I make one more home visit, Anthony shouldn't still be hanging out at his brother's house. The man has to work sometime to afford the way he lives."

"You aren't afraid to see him, are you?" Julie asked, and after the briefest hesitation added, "Are you afraid of him?"

"No, don't be silly," Mia said confidently. "It's only that I'm afraid it would be awkward."

But much later, after the call, when she lay in the dark seeking sleep, Mia remembered the moment she'd denied him and how he'd raced angrily into traffic. She remembered the feeling... and it was panic.

CHAPTER TWENTY-NINE

T uesday was, as Mia had predicted, an easy though busy day. She considered relaxing with her watercolors before leaving the hospital, but seeing how late it was sent her dashing into the bathroom to freshen up instead. It was almost time to meet Ron Bishop, and Mia was eager for the distraction. Before leaving, she scrolled to the picture she'd taken of her drawing of Ron's sister, Robin, and focused on the eyes.

As far back as high school, her art teacher had commended her on the skill with which she captured the life in her subjects' eyes, and when she looked into those of Robin on the page, Mia believed. *But it wasn't me.* Since this was a face she'd never seen, how could she take credit for capturing it?

Those eyes, those very familiar eyes, greeted her when she arrived at the Central Diner. Mia had been gratified when Ron suggested this destination. She was more familiar with the comfortable southside restaurant, and it was definitely more wallet friendly than LeMont.

Ron came to the door to meet her and led her back to a table where she saw he already had coffee.

"I didn't know what you liked to drink..." Ron said almost apologetically.

He had no idea how much Mia appreciated him not making any assumptions. After putting in her order for hot tea, she glanced through the expansive menu with which she was already fairly familiar and decided on the Central Burger. "I don't get burgers often," she said, "but they always look so good here." She substituted for sweet potato fries—her homage to eating healthy—and wondered if she'd have room left for cake.

Somewhat to her surprise, Mia felt completely at ease with the detective though they barely knew each other, and she had to laugh when Ron ordered the same burger, but with onion rings instead.

"I hope I have room left for cake," he said after handing his menu to the server.

Her puzzled look must have mystified the detective. When she explained, his eyes seemed to smile as much as his lips. Mia decided she liked his smile.

But his face soon became more serious. "Thank you for being willing to meet me. I think I should enlighten you on why your picture affected me so profoundly."

By the time their food arrived, he had shared the grim details of his parents' murder and sister's disappearance.

"So, you can imagine why suddenly seeing a picture that looks so much like Robin kind of freaked me out."

"But you said she disappeared when you... when she was only fifteen, and the picture I painted isn't a teenager. It's a woman. Yet you seem confident that's her?"

"I am," Ron said picking up an onion ring. "I wasn't sure I'd know her if I ran into her on the street. Now I know I would. I will."

Mia was surprised by how easily he had come to accept the validity of her drawing and how eagerly he was looking at her now.

"You told me how one of your drawings helped the police find the cabin where you were being held captive," he said. "But it sounded like that wasn't the only time something like this happened. Was it?"

"No," she replied, wondering how much to share. "A couple of years later, there was a little eight-year-old boy in our town who went missing. They feared the worst, of course, but after seeing the story on the news, I started drawing. It was different from when I drew the cabin—I didn't think there was anything that special then—but this time I knew it was important. There were a lot of trees and a stream, and a couple of big boulders. I knew it was connected to that little boy."

Mia studied Ron's face for signs of disbelief or skepticism, but seeing none she continued.

"There was an amber alert, and everyone was searching for him all day so my father called the police and told them we might be able to help. We were lucky. One of the detectives who showed up at our door was one of the same ones who'd been involved with my own disappearance... so he was willing to listen. Anyhow, he made copies and circulated the picture, showing it to all those involved in the search—just in case—and luckily there was a guy, a runner, who said he recognized the area." Mia could see Ron was hanging on every word, waiting. "And when this guy took them to that area, they found the little boy. And he was okay. He'd been missing for hours, and he was lost, hungry, cold, and terribly afraid." Mia remembered the feeling all too well. "But he was alive."

Ron hadn't moved, and when he didn't say anything, Mia thought perhaps he didn't believe her after all.

Their waitress stopped at the table and asked, "Can I get you any dessert or coffee?"

Ron looked across the table, and Mia watched a smile crawl across his face. Then with a wink he said, "I think I'll have a piece of that carrot cake this place is famous for, how about you?"

Mia let out her breath. "Yes, that sounds perfect," she answered. When the waitress left them alone again, she said, "So anyhow, there have only been a few other incidents, nothing quite that huge, but each time I have that unbeckoned urge to draw it's kind of like an itch I simply have to scratch."

Their cake was set on the table, and Ron glanced down at his plate then drew his eyes up to meet hers. "I have to tell you, last night I took your painting out, and I knew it was Robin. I couldn't stop looking at her, and after a while," he said lowering his voice, "I could almost hear her whispering, *Find me*'."

Chapter Thirty

A fter a few mouthfuls, Mia had to give up, but she watched with fascination as Ron finished every last bite of his carrot cake. He ate with unabandoned gusto, and when he finally dropped his fork onto the plate, he looked across the table sheepishly.

"I can't believe I finished it. Now you must think I'm a real hog."

Mia laughed. "No, I wish I could've eaten more, but I would've made myself sick. I'll just take it along home and have it later."

"More coffee?" the waitress asked, stopping by with a full pot. Ron nodded and smiled as she refilled his cup.

"Mine was tea," Mia said when the young woman turned to her.

"That's right... and would you like a box?" the waitress asked, nodding at the unfinished cake.

"Yes, please, and could I have another piece to go?"

Ron's eyebrows shot up.

"It's for my roommate," Mia explained. "She'd kill me if I brought this home and didn't have any for her."

As they lingered sipping their drinks, Ron grew serious again. "Mia, do you think you can help me find my sister?"

Mia wanted to help... wanted to help him... wished she could tell him what he wanted to hear.

"I don't know how," she said.

"It's been fifteen years since Robin disappeared." Mia heard the desperation in his voice. "I've followed every lead no matter how bogus. I refuse to believe she's... I mean I won't give up on her, but I don't have a c-clue." Ron's voice cracked. "Maybe you can draw something else... or do another painting that will tell us where she is?"

"I'm sorry, Ron. It doesn't work like that." Mia watched his shoulders slump. He looked so forlorn, she reached across the table and put her hand on his. "Okay, I, I'll try." She didn't really think there was much chance of it helping, but she was relieved to see the glimmer of hope return to his eyes.

When the waitress brought the check, Mia tried to pay her half, but Ron insisted on covering it. "But I wouldn't have ordered the extra cake if—"

"Stop. Don't worry about it," Ron said. "You're here because I asked for your help. The least I can do is pay for your meal."

"But I..."

"No buts." Ron shook his head and grinned, putting his credit card with the check.

Mia thanked him weakly and noticed the merriment dancing in his ever so blue eyes. But then she noticed something else going on. "What is it, Ron?"

"I was curious about something, but I don't know if I'm out of line asking."

Oh no, don't ruin this.

"It's about the Claire Alessi case."

Mia breathed a sigh of relief. Unsure what she'd expected, she was relieved to know it wasn't something more personal. "I'm not sure I know anything that could help with that."

"I understand, but I just thought maybe, you know, because of that picture you did with the earring... Well, was there anything else about that drawing that seemed kind of off to you? Or in any other drawings?"

Mia thought back, wanting to help, but she was certain there was nothing else she could tell him that would be any help. She shook her head. "There was just that speck of blue in the dirt... kind of looked like a sapphire with the sun making it sparkle. I can't think of anything else.

"Oh," Ron said, "and how about the other one—the one with the blue car?"

Mia shook her head again. "There weren't any others, and I don't know how I can help you."

It wasn't until much later that night, as she lay in bed trying to read her Bible passages that her mind kept straying back to the drawing. That blue car. Why was it blue? Could there actually have been a blue car in Freddie's garage that day? *Anthony's car is blue.*

Ron checked the time when his phone rang. Though he'd fallen asleep in his favorite chair it wasn't terribly late—just 10:30. Recognizing the caller ID, he answered quickly.

"I hope I didn't wake you," Mia said.

"No. I was just doing a little reading before heading in," Ron said tossing his unopened issue of *Guns and Ammo* aside. "What's up?"

"It's probably nothing, but I couldn't stop thinking about Freddie's drawing and the blue car in my painting, and um, well, it occurred to me Freddie's brother drives a blue Tesla. I mean, lots of people drive blue cars but I..."

Ron heard the hesitancy in her voice. "Yeah, lots of people drive blue cars, Mia, but lots of people weren't there to bring Freddie to the hospital."

"But Anthony explained how he happened to be driving by..."

"Sure, of course you're right. It's probably nothing, but I'm glad you called. It's my job to follow every lead, and you never know which one will give you the answers you're looking for." Ron wanted to say more. Wanted to keep her on the phone simply to hear the soothing sound of her voice.

"Okay, well..."

"Mia, wait, don't hang up," Ron said grasping for something to say. "I, I just wanted to thank you again for having dinner with me, and for giving me hope again. I mean about Robin."

Mia assured him she was happy to help if she could, so he took a gamble. "Well, maybe we could do it again sometime?"

"Sure," she said.

"Oh, and I forgot to tell you. That guy, Mason? He's not our man. He had a solid alibi for the night of Claire's murder. But he's definitely a bully and probably worse."

Unable to think of anything else, he ended the call then sat contemplating all the events of the evening. He had enjoyed spending time with this young woman for whom he had such an inexplicable attraction. And then there was her gift. It all sounded too incredible to believe, yet he knew it was true. Her painting of Robin was proof, wasn't it? Whether it was a gift from God, as she seemed to believe, or some kind of unimaginable intuition, it didn't matter. All the doubt that crept into his mind in recent years was instantly erased. Robin had lived and grown older just like he had... somewhere. *I promise, I will find you, Robin.*

CHAPTER THIRTY-ONE

R on hadn't planned on making another trip out to the Alessi place, but a cryptic call from Freddie seemed pretty urgent. When he pulled into the empty driveway, it occurred to him it was the first time Anthony's car wasn't there. It was also obvious that no one was bothering to take care of the lawn while the homeowner was incapacitated.

The front door opened even before he reached it, and Freddie waved him in, then led the way to the living room. Ron was impressed by the speed with which Freddie swung his crutches and hopped along. "You're moving pretty good there, " Ron said to start the conversation.

"Yeah, and I can take care of myself pretty damn well, too." He flopped down on the couch where he apparently spent most of his time these days. "But I can't seem to convince my brother of that."

Freddie pushed his laptop to the side of the coffee table, but from what Ron saw on the screen, he could tell Freddie wasn't using it to play games. And the glass on the end table didn't look like iced tea. Scotch on the rocks maybe?

"So, is Anthony here now?"

"No, I asked him to run some errands for me. I can get around the house all right, but I can't push a cart around some grocery store, and Claire's…" Freddie cleared his throat. "She always did the shopping," he said, voice drifting off. After clearing his throat again, he said gruffly, "That's why I asked if you could come right away."

Ron's curiosity was piqued. "Why's that?"

"Because what I have to say is just between the two of us, at least for now. The thing is, I remembered something, and it's about Anthony."

Ron moved to the edge of his seat. He pulled the notepad out of his pocket and waited.

"He was here," Freddie said almost in a whisper.

"You mean when you came to?"

"No, he was here when I got home from the office." Freddie rubbed the back of his neck, and Ron noticed his quickened breathing. "I opened the garage to pull in, but his car was already in there. I couldn't imagine why. I vaguely remember being scared. I guess I thought something had happened to Claire." He looked up at Ron and shrugged. "But she hadn't called me. I'm sure of it."

"So, what happened next?"

"I remember I rushed into the house, and called out their names. It was quiet. I sprinted up the steps." Freddie slumped back into the cushions.

Ron waited, but Freddie now seemed miles away. "Then what happened?" he asked.

Freddie's head came up and he looked at the detective wide eyed. "I don't know," he said. "That's all I can remember." He shook his head, and his eyes narrowed. "But I know this for sure. My brother was already in the house when I got here."

"Freddie, do you think Anthony could have been the one who pushed you down the steps? Do you think he did something to Claire?"

They both turned at the sound of the front door opening. They hadn't heard the near-silent electric motor of the Tesla.

"Hey, Detective. What brings you here again this morning?" Anthony asked, heaving a sigh Ron heard as annoyed... or perhaps unsettled?

"He just dropped in to see if I'd remembered anything else," Freddie said quickly with a sidelong glance at Ron.

"Again?" Anthony said. "Any luck, Detective?"

Ron looked at Anthony, turned to Freddie—whose expression begged his confidence—then back to the older brother. "No, not yet," he said, "but you never know..." He quietly slipped his notepad into his pocket and got to his feet.

"You're back fast," Freddie said to his brother. "Did you get everything?"

"I got all the groceries on your list," Anthony said, "but the line at the pharmacy was ridiculous. I can run back there after lunch."

"You know what? There's nothing else I need that can't wait 'til tomorrow, so if you've got other things to do, you can go."

"Don't be silly. I'm in no hurry. I'll fix us some lunch first. Is there anything else, Detective?"

"No, Anthony," Ron said turning to Freddie, "unless you've thought of something." Freddie assured him he hadn't, so Ron decided to follow the other man's lead until he had more to go on. "Okay, I'm gonna head out. If you think of anything, you know how to reach me."

Anthony followed him to the door and out onto the front porch. "I wish you'd leave my brother alone now. It's obvious he's not going to remember what happened, so maybe you should do your job and look elsewhere."

Ron bristled, but was unwilling to put his cards on the table before he knew he had a winning hand. Instead he just smiled. "See you later, Anthony."

On the way to his vehicle, he eyed Anthony's blue car. *No wonder he's so concerned about what his little brother remembers.*

Checking his calls, he saw he'd missed three, but there was only one that mattered. The caller ID simply said Mia.

CHAPTER THIRTY-TWO

Mia sat in the solarium soaking in the sunlight. When she'd chosen this apartment in South Side, it was mainly because of the light in this room directly off her bedroom. Mia couldn't imagine a better art space, and fortunately, Morgan said all she needed was a decent kitchen and a place to sleep. The second bedroom suited her fine. And the windowsill of the solarium certainly suited Simeon. He kept watch on the neighborhood, glancing back at Mia only occasionally.

Mia knew having a roommate would make it a lot easier to afford such a nice apartment. She hadn't known how much more Morgan would be than someone with whom to share the expenses. It was almost like having another sister, and this one was close enough to hug. Having left the bedroom door open after getting her morning tea, Mia wasn't surprised when Morgan wandered in.

"I see Simmie is enjoying the sun this morning. What are you up to, roomie?" Morgan asked, Yeti mug in hand. "Any plans for the day?"

"I think I'm just going to hang out here for a while. I've kind of got an itch to get something down," Mia said looking at the blank paper in front of her. "Are you going somewhere?"

"Yeah, just goin' for a stroll. I'm covering for Pam from three to eleven today so I've gotta get my fresh air this morning. I'll probably stop and grab an early lunch. Want me to bring you anything?"

Mia declined the offer. She wasn't hungry even though she'd skipped breakfast.

"Okay," Morgan said bending down to give Mia a little hug. "But call me if you change your mind. You've gotta eat, yanno!"

Mia assured her roommate she was in no danger of starving, then put Morgan and any idea of eating out of mind to focus on wetting the paper in front of her. She picked up her green pencil and began doodling a landscape of shrubs and trees. Grabbing first a yellow, then pink, then purple she worked quickly and soon there were lovely wildflowers scattered over the ground. The addition of several shades of blue and pink, with white space showing the light, brought out an early evening summer sky with mountains in the distant background.

"Wow."

Mia jumped at the voice right behind her. She hadn't been aware of the time passing.

Morgan laughed. "Sorry, I didn't mean to startle you. But that's gorgeous, girl. You're so talented. Where is that?"

"Thank you." Mia warmed at the kind words. She'd heard them many times before from many people, and she was so grateful for the gift she'd been given. "But it's just a landscape... nowhere specific."

"Really? Wow... so did you eat yet?"

Mia realized she was hungry after all and checked the time. Or was it the aroma drifting from the bag Morgan was holding that made her stomach growl?

"I haven't, no. I smell fries," she said spinning around.

"Yes, ma'am. The way you've been moping around, I figured you'd forget to eat so I brought you a sandwich and fries. You can have the burger or the BLT."

"I'm not moping... and I'll have the BLT."

"Yeah, you kind of are," Morgan said leading the way to the kitchen. "I hope you're not still brooding over that chump. He's not worth it."

Mia grabbed a plate for herself—Morgan always ate hers right from the wrapper—and loaded it with half the sandwich and some fries while considering her roommate's words.

"No, I'm not actually *brooding* over Anthony. But it was kind of exciting having someone like him interested, you know?"

"You can do better."

Mia thought about that and knew Morgan was right. But after the last couple years of having no one special—ever since the breakup with her college sweetheart—it had felt good to be held. To be kissed. If Anthony just hadn't wanted, tried to insist, on more.

Later, after Morgan left for the hospital, Mia went for a long walk trying to fight off her malaise. It didn't work. Although she loved historic South Side, her walk didn't have the usual effect of lifting her mood. The sun was still high in the sky when she returned to her apartment, but her energy was zapped.

Falling into the big brown beast, she let her mind drift. When Ron Bishop had returned her call Thursday, she'd asked him about Anthony... if he thought the brother could have actually been involved with Claire Alessi's murder. Ron said he couldn't really comment since it was still an open investigation, but then added that Anthony was a *person of interest*. Mia hadn't shared that piece of information with Morgan. And she hadn't heard anything more from the detective.

Unable to sit still any longer, Mia went to the kitchen, opened the refrigerator, stared at its contents, then closed it again. She wandered into her bedroom, then was drawn out to the solarium and the picture she'd painted a few hours earlier. She was satisfied with it. It was simple yet special. Almost in a trance, she stared at the watercolor and the minutes passed. She felt the image drawing her in.

When the phone rang, she knew without looking that it was him. "Hello, Ron."

CHAPTER THIRTY-THREE

Freddie grabbed his crutches and hobbled over to the front window. He watched his brother back out of the driveway and speed off down the road entirely too fast. But then, Freddie wondered, why should Anthony have to drive within the speed limit? His brother had never felt the need to follow directions, procedures, or guidelines if it didn't suit his purpose. Not at home or school or anywhere else. Freddie thought about all the times Anthony had disregarded the rules and gotten away with it. *But was he capable of murder?*

He hobbled back to his usual spot on the couch—totally exhausted—picked up his phone and the detective's business card, and punched in the number.

"Yeah, I think I remember something else," Freddie said. "Can you come by?"

His leg was throbbing, and he knew his earlier escapade was at least partially to blame, but he had needed to go upstairs. He hadn't been up there since that night, and the compulsion couldn't be denied.

A loud banging on the door sent him grabbing for his crutches and pushing himself up. He hadn't meant to doze off and felt somewhat disoriented as he rushed to the door. Someone was obviously trying to bust it down.

"Yeah, yeah, I'm coming," he shouted.

"Sorry, but I knocked and rang the bell," the detective said. "And when you didn't answer, I thought something might have happened."

Freddie led the man to the living room and collapsed back onto the couch, explaining he'd fallen asleep.

"So, Freddie, you said you remembered more about the day your wife was killed?"

"Yeah... I went upstairs today."

He saw Ron's jaw drop.

"I know, it was kind of crazy," Freddie continued, "but I hadn't been up there since, you know... and I had to."

"But how did you manage?" Ron asked glancing out at the long stairway.

"Motivation," Freddie said with a wink. "It took a while going up on my butt and dragging the crutches. I was almost to the top, when I lost one of them. Watched it slide the whole way back down the damn steps. I thought of going after it, but I knew my brother was coming over—like he does every damn day—and I wanted to finish what I was doing and get back down here before he could."

"Just what was it you wanted to do?"

"I'm getting to that. So anyhow, I just swore and dragged myself up the last few steps. Next was the hard part. Did you ever try to stand up from a sitting position with a broken leg and one crutch?"

"Can't say I have."

"Well don't," Freddie said rolling his eyes. "I was sweatin' bullets by the time I did, and damn lucky I didn't fall back down those damn steps." Freddie leaned back against the sofa cushions and sighed. "But I got it done. Somehow, I got to the bedroom. Our bedroom. The door was open," he paused remembering, then locked eyes with Ron. "I remember."

"What? What do you remember?"

"I remember hearing them. Claire wasn't alone. My brother was there. Anthony was there with her."

"I'm sorry," Ron muttered. Then after several moments passed in silence, he prompted, "Freddie..."

"Oh yeah." He'd almost forgotten the detective was there. "So..." He couldn't think what else to say. Finally, leaning forward, he said, "I can't believe it, but..." Freddie's voice trailed off. No, he couldn't believe it, but it was true. He remembered seeing Anthony. Seeing the shock on his brother's face.

"Do you think they were having an affair?"

"No!" Freddie gripped the crutch he'd had leaning on the couch next to him and threw it to the floor. "I think my brother wanted something and just decided to take it." His eyes squeezed shut to block out the image. "Claire would never... no, that's Anthony. He takes what he wants. No matter who it hurts. I should probably warn my therapist."

Ron's head jerked up. "What do you mean?"

"He took her out a couple times. But I think she's done with him. He didn't seem any too happy about it either. Anyhow, I'm pretty sure she saw through all his so-called charm and dumped him."

***

Ron watched Freddie's face morph. Saw the fury behind his eyes. Knew he'd never be able to hide that kind of anger from his brother. "Did you tell Anthony what you remembered?"

"No," Freddie answered.

Ron saw the pulsing vein at his temple and waited for more.

"I... I didn't say much of anything. Just told him I didn't need him hanging around." Freddie sneered. "I told him to get out. And when I knew he was gone, I called you."

"So, you don't think he has any idea?" Ron had been a detective too long to think it was that simple. "Do you think he's going to come back here?"

"No, at least not for a while. He was pretty pissed when he left." Freddie's head dropped, and he pulled his hands through already disheveled hair. He reeked with the smell of anxiety and exhaustion. Then he slowly lifted his eyes to meet Ron's. "My God, Bishop, I don't want to believe it, but I think he killed her. My own brother killed my Claire."

CHAPTER THIRTY-FOUR

"Row, row, row your boat, gently down the stream," Mia sang softly. She sat facing Mrs. Lillian Perry, holding her patient's hands, swinging them left to right as she sang. This warm-up exercise brought her patient back to the moment, and it wasn't long before Mrs. Perry was singing along, remembering every word of the old familiar tune.

When Mia switched to "Daisy, Daisy, give me your answer do..." Lillian Perry apparently recognized Mia. She knew where she was, and gradually became more aware, more relaxed, and ready to join in the activity that always gave her pleasure.

Lillian drew flowers and colored them red and purple. Before long, she had cut out all the paper blooms and glued them in a pleasing arrangement.

"Your flowers are lovely," Mia said.

"I used to have such beautiful ones, you know. I loved my daylilies, especially the Ruby Throat. My son, my Sammy, gave me my first one on Mother's Day—the first Mother's Day after he got married," Mrs. Perry said.

Mia appreciated the relaxed smile on her patient's face as she reminisced. Seeing how creating art brought life back into her dementia patients, she knew she'd chosen the right profession for herself.

When Mrs. Perry finished gluing her red flowers on the paper, she began adding the others.

"And what are these delightful purple ones?" Mia asked.

"Oh, that's echinacea, my purple coneflower, dear." Mrs. Perry went on talking about the various flowers in her gardens, and Mia stayed with her—stayed in the moment—but something was lurking in the back of her mind, begging for her attention.

At the end of their session, Mia wheeled her patient back to her room and hung the picture of the red and purple garden on the little bulletin board for her to enjoy.

"I'll see you next week, Lil," Mia said.

"All right, Barbie," Mrs. Perry answered. "Hug those grandbabies for me."

"Okay, I will," Mia answered, realizing her patient's fleeting moments of being fully aware and in the present had already slipped away. When Mia had first started working with dementia patients, she would try to correct them—try to make them recognize who she was—but she'd learned. Now when Mrs. Perry thought her daughter was there to visit, Mia knew it was okay to give her that rather than contradict her.

As she headed to the door, Mia glanced at the purple coneflowers her patient had so lovingly glued to the paper, then recognized what had been calling for her attention. These flowers were familiar for a reason. She couldn't wait to get home and examine it to be sure, but these were almost certainly the same kind she'd painted in her landscape.

First, though, she had to stop back at the hospital to finish up her file notes, check her schedule for Tuesday, and do any necessary prep. She didn't see Morgan on her way in, but her roommate was at the nurses' station charting when Mia headed for the exit.

"See you at home," Morgan called quietly. "Should I stop and grab us something for dinner on the way?"

"No, I took those shrimp out of the freezer this morning. I was planning on making stir-fry if that's all right with you."

"Excellent! You know I love me some home cooking... as long as I don't have to be the cook."

Mia laughed. She knew Morgan would eat out or order in every night of the week rather than cook. That's why she'd taken on the role of chef while Morgan would usually do clean up.

A sudden spring shower met Mia when she got outside. As her windshield wipers intermittently cleared the glass, Mia hoped the light rain would stop soon enough for her to take a walk before dinner.

Forty-five minutes after leaving Mrs. Perry, Mia arrived home, and went directly to the solarium to inspect the purple flowers she'd painted. *Echinacea,* her patient had called them, and these were definitely the same purple coneflowers. Satisfied she'd been correct, she glanced out the window to be sure the brief afternoon shower had passed, then changed into her walking shoes and headed out for a little exercise.

Mia inhaled the fresh smell of springtime and stopped for just a minute to enjoy the rainbow. Heading down Carson to Tenth St., every step brought new visions of her favorite season. This was the time of year that filled her artist's soul with longing to put paint to canvas, but her mission at the moment was exercise, so she quickened her steps with intermittent jogging until she got to the river.

The sun had returned with a vengeance, and when she reached the Monongahela River, she slowed her pace and let the gentle breeze cool her dampened skin. On the way home, there was no jogging. She had learned to see the beauty all around her. It's something she shared with her sister who was also an artist. Julie just painted with words instead of watercolors.

Mia was so engrossed with the splendor of her surroundings, she hadn't noticed the blue Tesla following her until she neared her apartment building and it pulled up to the curb beside her.

Anthony leapt out and circled the front of the car. "Get in," he said opening the passenger door.

"Excuse me?" Mia gawked at his impudence. "You've got to be kidding." But she could see he wasn't.

"Get in, Mia... please... I just want to talk."

He must be crazy. But he said he just wants to talk. Mia's mind raced. *But last time...* "I don't think so, Anthony."

"Why not?"

She couldn't believe he'd even ask. "Because the last time you drove like a maniac and scared me half to death."

"Yeah, okay, but I promise that won't happen again. Scout's honor," he said raising his hand right hand.

"Anthony, it doesn't matter. I told you, this—you and me—it isn't going to work."

"I'm not asking you out, Mia. Please... I just need to talk to you *about Freddie!*"

Mia looked into his brown eyes, those same eyes that had attracted her from the first time she'd looked into them, and she wished it could be different. Knew it couldn't be. But the soft side of Mia found it hard to deny him the chance to at least explain himself.

She hesitated just a moment longer, then got into the car.

CHAPTER THIRTY-FIVE

*I*s it enough for a conviction? Ron went over and over the facts before him. There was no longer any doubt in his mind. He was convinced Anthony had killed his sister-in-law. But there were still some unanswered questions. Was he having an affair with Claire? Probably. Or did he attack her, taking her against her will? Maybe. But it was apparent Freddie walked in on them. He had either caught his brother standing over Claire's dead body, or he caught them in the act. And until Freddie got the rest of his memory back, they might never know. Either way, Anthony was responsible. He'd assaulted his brother and killed Claire. But how to prove it without a shadow of doubt?

Ron knew what he needed. *A confession.*

He checked the address Freddie had given him for his brother. *Pretty fancy place for somebody who never seems to work*, Ron thought when he arrived, but unfortunately, Anthony wasn't there.

Checking the other address he'd gotten from Freddie, Ron headed to an office in one of the most reputable banking establishments downtown. *An investment banker—no wonder he's rolling in it.*

Freddie had told Ron that Anthony was a Managing Director so Ron wasn't too surprised by the receptionist's first question. "Do you have an appointment?"

Ron pulled out his badge, certain that would get him in to see "the boss" regardless of not having an appointment in the book.

"I'm sorry, Detective Bishop, but Mr. Alessi isn't here right now."

"When will he be back?"

The receptionist looked down at the schedule. "He had a late lunch meeting with an important client, but he has no other appointments this afternoon. I don't know if he'll be back in today."

Handing the young woman his card, Ron said, "Call me if he does return, or if you hear from him. I have a few questions I'm hoping he can help me with."

Once back in his car, he punched Freddie's number into his phone. No luck. Anthony hadn't gone back there. *Just as well.* "Call or text me if he does come back or if you hear from him."

Ron found himself cruising the city streets, always watching for the blue Tesla, while trying to decide his next step.

Anthony was nobody's fool, so Ron would have to be careful just how to handle the man. He could put out an APB, but he wasn't ready to arrest him. Not yet. And he was counting on something else—the one good thing on his side. No matter how clever, the bad guys usually managed to slip up somewhere.

Eventually the detective found himself in South Side and turned on Carson Street. He thought of Mia and remembered what Freddie said. *"He takes what he wants. No matter who it hurts."*

With a sudden sense of urgency, he parked and hurriedly went to Mia's apartment door. He was relieved to hear movement inside, but his heart dropped when Morgan—a nurse he'd met at the hospital—opened the door. Mia had mentioned they were roommates.

"Detective Bishop," Morgan said eyes wide. "What are you doing here? I mean has something happened?"

Ron wondered why people always seemed alarmed when he showed up at their door. He didn't *always* have bad news.

"Hello, Morgan. Is Mia here?"

"No, has something happened to her?"

He saw fear in the nurse's eyes. "What do you mean? Why do you think something's happened?"

"No, sorry, I overreacted," Morgan said. "Come in and sit down. She should be back soon."

Ron took the offered seat but never took his eyes off Morgan who was checking out the window.

"Do you know where she is?"

"No, but I know she's gotta be back shortly."

"What makes you think so?"

"The shrimp," Morgan answered quickly.

"What?"

"The shrimp," she repeated and then laughed at herself. "Mia said she was making shrimp stir-fry for dinner, so I know she's not going out to eat with him."

"With who?" Ron asked warily.

"Just this guy, Anthony. Oh, that's right, you've met him. He's the brother of that patient whose wife was killed." Ron saw her eyes darting toward the window. "He's a bit of a jerk. And I know she had a better time when she had dinner with you."

"Really? She said that?" Ron felt the smile he couldn't keep from curling his lips. But then he considered the rest of it. Mia had gotten in the car with Anthony? *Why?*

The more Ron mulled it over, the more uneasy he became. "Mia didn't say anything about going out with him tonight then?"

"No, like I said, she told me not to pick up dinner because she had it covered... the stir-fry. That's why I was surprised to see her get in his car."

Alarms went off in Ron's mind. "Today? You saw her with Anthony Alessi today?"

"Yeah, I saw them driving away when I was pulling in. I was shocked, actually. I mean Mia told me she was done with him. He's a real jackass." Ron squinted his eyes and pressed his lips together. "I'm sorry, but he is," she added.

"You don't need to apologize," Ron said bolting to his feet. "But I've been looking for Anthony. Do you have any idea where they might have gone?"

"No. What's going on? Why are you looking for him anyway?"

"I just have some questions about the sister-in-law's case, and it's important I talk to Mia too."

At that moment he looked out the window and watched the sun disappear. Unlike the earlier spring shower, this purple sky signaled it was going to be a real storm. Much like the one he felt brewing inside.

"Morgan, think. Do you have any idea where they might have gone?" he asked frantically.

"No... I mean, they only went out a few times. Once he took her to a fancy place... um, LeMont. And then there was the Italian restaurant, but like I said, I'm sure she's not going to go to dinner with him." Morgan rubbed her forehead. "He... um, he did take her to his place once, but I don't know where that is..."

Ron didn't like hearing that, but he needed to check it out. "I know where it is. Listen, if she calls or if... I mean, when she gets back, would you give me a call?" He handed Morgan his card and was almost out the door before she stopped him.

"Oh, and I forgot. Mia told me about this scenic overlook where he liked to go, though I know she wouldn't want to go back there with him."

"But she's not the one driving, right? Do you know where it is?"

Morgan told him more about the spot, and he knew exactly where it was.

"Thanks," he called over his shoulder dashing out the door and down the hall.

I've got to find her.

But he kept hearing Freddie's words. "*He takes what he wants. No matter who it hurts.*"

CHAPTER THIRTY-SIX

Mia was relieved that Anthony was true to his word—at least so far—driving the speed limit. He hadn't said anything since they pulled away from the curb.

"Anthony." Mia's voice was barely above a whisper. "What's going on?"

He glanced her way, then back at the road.

"What do you want from me, Anthony? I told you this... this whatever it is that's going on between us, just isn't going to work for me."

He gave her another sidelong glance, and she could see the vein in his temple throbbing. Filled with a slow-growing dread, she remembered another time she'd foolishly gotten into a car—that time with a stranger who'd lied about his identity—and she'd wound up locked in a cage. But she had been a silly, naïve adolescent then. Now as a grown woman, she chided herself for being such a fool. *What am I doing?*

Mia jumped when he finally spoke.

"Listen, I'm not coming on to you, okay?" he said. "I only want to talk."

"What do we have to talk about?"

"Not about us. You've made yourself quite clear on that topic," he said. "And trust me, you're not breaking my heart."

Mia was taken aback and unsure whether she was more relieved or insulted.

"Then what?" she asked unable to think clearly.

"Freddie."

"What about Freddie? I didn't even see him today." None of this was making any sense, unless... "Is something wrong? I mean he canceled today's session, but I didn't sense he was sick or anything. Is he?" Mia fell back into the role of therapist and feared for her patient.

"He's fine," Anthony snapped.

When he didn't go on, Mia snapped back. "Then what?" Her patience was running thin, and seeing where he was taking them didn't help.

Anthony pulled on the brake at what was apparently his favorite spot. A spot with a view she remembered delighting in the first time he'd brought her there. That fairytale night when his kiss had promised so much more. But perhaps also a spot where his prey was trapped.

Mia felt herself draw back when he turned toward her. Gripped by fear, her mind flashed back to the last time she'd been in this car... the flat tire... the dirt in the trunk...

"You don't need to act like I'm gonna bite," he said with obvious disgust. "Trust me, if I wanted you, you'd be mine, little girl."

Mia's cheeks burned at the insult. "I am not a ch-child," she said, infuriated that her voice cracked as she said it. "Take me home!"

Anthony's eyes widened, but he didn't make a move toward starting the car. Finally, she saw it... she remembered what she hadn't seen clearly at the time. There in the dirty trunk, the sun had glistened off something. *The missing earring!*

"Fine," she said voice trembling. "I'll walk if I have to. Or maybe you can call me an Uber again. You're pretty good at that."

"Knock it off!" he yelled, scaring her into temporary submission. "Look, I'm worried," he said more gently. "I need to know what's going on with my brother."

"What do you mean?" *He's afraid Freddie will remember. Oh God...*

"He's been acting more and more erratic, and he gets so angry. I mean like his temper is out of control."

"I guess it runs in the family," Mia said but quickly pressed her lips together when she saw the darkness in Anthony's glare. She knew she shouldn't antagonize him. *My God, he's a murderer.*

"I'm not kidding here. I'm concerned by how agitated he gets."

"Okay, but what's that got to do with me?"

"Well, he talks to you. And I thought you might know... Is his memory of the night, the night Claire was killed... is he remembering more about what happened?"

"No. I mean... I don't know." Mia's breath came faster. She couldn't let him know what she was thinking. "He hasn't said anything to me about it."

"Yeah, I was thinking maybe if he remembered whoever broke in... maybe remembered the guy pushing him down the steps... he might've said something to you..."

"No, no, he hasn't said a thing." That part was true. "Besides, I should think you'd want him to remember, so maybe he could identify the..." Mia stopped herself and shifted. "Maybe then he could have peace of mind."

Mia felt her phone vibrate in her pocket but let it go to voicemail and continued watching Anthony's face.

After several seconds of glowering at her, he replaced the glare with his mask of compassion. "Yeah," was all he said before starting the ignition and pulling back onto the road.

Relieved the whole terrifying ordeal was ending, Mia made a quick check of her phone. She saw a missed call from Ron Bishop and a text message that made the hair stand up on the back of her neck.

Anthony Alessi may be dangerous. Get away from him asap.

She quickly texted back:

He has missing earring.

Ron's reply was almost instant:

Where are you?

"What are you doing?" Anthony asked glimpsing the phone in her hand.

"Just checking my messages. Morgan is wondering where I am," she lied hoping he didn't hear the quiver in her voice. "I told her I was making dinner tonight, and she's getting hungry. I'll just let her know I'm on my way."

"Don't!" he said firmly clamping his hand over hers.

Mia wanted to answer Ron's message but couldn't. She did manage to push the home button and hide the text. *It's all right. I'll be home soon.*

But she was so wrong.

Mia watched Anthony's vein still throbbing at his temple and noticed his tightly clenched jaw. That's when the threatening storm let loose and there was a sudden downpour. *"He might be dangerous."* Ron's text had done nothing to alleviate her sense of dread. She wanted to let the detective know where she was.

When Anthony's hold had loosened, she moved to look at the phone again. She turned it over and placed her thumb to unlock it, and opened her text messages. Anthony quickly snatched it away from her.

"What's so important?" he asked gruffly while steering with his left hand and holding the phone in his right. "Shit." He threw the phone over his right shoulder into the backseat and glowered at her. "I am not dangerous! And you don't know what you're talking about. I don't have any damn earring!"

Mia thought his tone didn't match his words, and when he turned the opposite direction from her apartment, she recognized the same alarm she'd had years ago when another man had headed down a country road to hold her captive for days.

She considered jumping out of the car if he stopped at a red light but wasn't sure how long it would take to remove the seat belt and get out.

It didn't matter. They were having the kind of luck you only dream of when you're running late. Every light turned green before they reached it... until he turned onto a familiar route.

They were heading to Freddie Alessi's house. *But why?*

CHAPTER THIRTY-SEVEN

Ron's heart pounded like the constant beating of the windshield wipers racing madly back and forth struggling to clear his view. They were failing miserably. With no sign of the blue Tesla at the scenic spot Morgan had told him about, he hit the switches for the light and sirens, and cautiously pulled back into traffic. With sheets of rain reducing visibility, he couldn't take any chances. He couldn't even count on the siren not being drowned out by the rain pounding other drivers' cars. But he had to get to Alessi's apartment.

He punched the number he'd put in his phone before leaving Mia's place. "Hey... no, I haven't found them yet," he told Morgan. "So you haven't heard anything either?" He realized he probably shouldn't be shouting into the phone, but it was the only way to hear himself. After filling Morgan in on his next step, he hung up and put his full attention on the road and rushed to the plush apartment building he'd visited earlier.

No answer when he pounded on the door. Even though he hadn't seen Anthony's car in the garage, he got management to open the door. He had to be certain.

The apartment was empty, and there were no signs anyone had recently been there. A half-drained single coffee mug was the only sign anyone even lived there, and the beverage was cold. No evidence of breakfast or lunch, but then Ron couldn't imagine Anthony Alessi standing over a frying pan of bacon and eggs.

Ron verbally identified himself to anyone who might be in the bedroom, then opened the door to find nothing but an unmade bed.

Back in the great room, he looked around, mind racing. He pulled out his phone and tried Mia's number again. No answer. Every detective's instinct told him Mia was in danger, and he couldn't let anything happen to her. He no longer doubted Anthony had killed once. *Would he kill again?*

Moments later he was sitting in his car with the motor running but no idea where to go. He hammered the steering wheel with both fists. *Where are you, Mia?*

He put the car in gear and pulled out of the parking garage relieved the monsoon had ebbed to a steady downpour.

Hearing the familiar hum, Ron snatched his phone from the console, but the caller ID wasn't the one he'd hoped for.

"Yeah, Freddie. What's up? Did you remember something else?"

Ron listened, and pushed the gas pedal to the floor at Freddie's next words. "No, but I think you might want to get over here. Anthony just pulled up. He's getting out of the car... and he's got Mia Reed with him."

CHAPTER THIRTY-EIGHT

The rain had let up a little, but Mia was still drenched by the time Anthony dragged her from the car to Freddie's front door. "Why did you bring me here?" she demanded while Anthony banged for entrance.

He didn't answer her. He just pushed her through the threshold when Freddie finally answered the door.

"What the hell?" Freddie's brows were drawn so close they nearly met in the middle. "What do you want?" he asked looking from Mia to his brother and back.

Mia wasn't sure if she read more anger or fear on his face. She settled on fear, and wondered if her own face exhibited the terror growing in her gut.

She silently rebuked herself for not putting it all together sooner. The blue car in the garage—it was him! Anthony killed his brother's wife. And now here she was right in the middle of things. Yet, she couldn't believe he would cold-bloodedly kill his own brother... and her.

"Anthony—"

"Be quiet, Mia." Anthony half shoved her across the room and she fell onto the couch.

Freddie dropped onto the other end, in his usual spot, and looked at her warily.

"All right, Anthony," he said. "What's going on here?"

"That's what I want to know, little brother."

"What do you mean? I'm here minding my own business, and you come barging in with my therapist..."

"This morning, when you were in such a mood," Anthony said perching on the edge of the chair on the other side of the room—the same chair Mia had taken the first time she'd come to this house, "something was up. You know it, and so do I. You

159

remember, don't you? Did you tell her?" Anthony nodded in Mia's direction. "And why do you keep looking out the window?"

"I'm not! I mean... the rain, the storm, that's all."

"The hell with the rain—answer my question. Do you remember what happened or not?"

"All right, yes. I remember," Freddie shouted. "You killed her, didn't you?" It wasn't so much a question as an accusation. "You killed my Claire, you sonofabitch!"

Mia's jaw dropped and she sucked in her breath as Anthony jumped out of the chair. Freddie had confirmed what she already knew to be true. Her mind raced to what would happen next. *Oh God, and now I know.* Was he going to kill them both? *Why did he want me here?* Then came the words from somewhere deep within, *"Trust in the Lord."*

She very slowly let her breath out when she saw Ron standing in the doorway to the hall. But then her eyes moved to Anthony's face filled with shock... and something else.

"What the... *NO!*" Anthony yelled. "I didn't kill her."

Ron stood back a few yards. He hadn't said a word, but Mia saw his hand on the gun she'd never noticed before.

"Are you crazy?" Anthony continued. "I thought you said you remembered."

"I did. I do remember. I came home and found you with her. Why? Why did you do it?"

Mia saw Freddie's eyes fill with tears. She wanted to go to him. To comfort him. She was afraid, but she had to do something. She reached across and put her hand on his arm. "Freddie, I'm so sorry." She couldn't imagine what he was going through knowing his own brother was the one who had destroyed his life.

She glared at Anthony, but something wasn't right.

"Freddie," he said sharply. "You have to know I didn't kill her."

"Anthony Alessi," came a voice from behind him. "You're under arrest for the murder of Claire Alessi," Ron said calmly.

"*NO!* I didn't kill her!" Anthony spun and backed away.

"But I saw you!" Freddie accused.

"Well, you didn't see me kill her. You couldn't have... because I didn't do it."

Ron took a step toward Anthony.

"Ron, wait," Mia said. "Freddie, exactly what do you remember?"

Freddie looked from her to his brother.

"No, Freddie, look at me," she said. "Now take a breath and tell me exactly what you remember."

A quick peek showed her that Ron and Anthony had both stopped and were watching her.

"I came home from the office, and Anthony's car was in my spot in the garage." Freddie spoke almost as if in a trance. "I panicked. Thought something must have happened."

"And then what..." Mia prompted.

"I... I ran in the house... and it was quiet. There was no sign of anything wrong downstairs, so I dashed upstairs thinking Claire must be sick or hurt or something, you know?"

Keeping her voice as serene as possible, Mia asked, "Yes, and what did you find? Was Anthony there?"

"Yes, in the bedroom... with Claire." Freddie's head spun around, and he shot a deadly look at his brother. Had he not been injured, Mia was sure he would have attacked his brother in that moment.

"But I didn't kill her, Freddie!" Anthony yelled. "You have to know that. I *loved* her!"

Silence.

Then he whispered, "I was *in love* with her."

No one else spoke in the seconds that followed—seconds that felt like hours.

Though stunned, Mia knew she had to keep going. Composing herself, she slid closer to Freddie, put her hand on his cheek, and turned his face to her. "Freddie, look at me... breathe. Now think. Look at Claire... Exactly what do you see?" She waited and saw her patient's expression slowly morph. The anger drained away to be replaced by shock.

"No," he murmured. His head sluggishly turned back so he could face his brother, but he still spoke as if he were talking to Claire. "He was in bed with her." His next words were aimed at Anthony. "You were in bed with my wife!" Eyes now filled with fury, he pushed himself up, grabbing for his crutches. He dropped one and swung the other, missing Anthony by inches. "You bastard!"

Ron took a step forward but stopped when Mia put up a hand.

"But I didn't kill her," Anthony insisted. "Think, Freddie. You have to remember. You screamed and threatened to kill me. You grabbed the baseball bat you kept by the bed and came at me, screaming for me to get out. So, I left, Freddie... I left."

Mia knew Anthony was telling the truth. He was a cad, but it was starting to become clear. Mia knew he hadn't killed Claire Alessi.

CHAPTER THIRTY-NINE

Ron relaxed the grip on his gun and let his hand fall to his side, but he was ever vigilant. He only took his eyes off Anthony fleetingly to check on Mia. He was astounded by her calm and the way she was managing the situation.

Freddie hadn't spoken since Anthony swore he'd left the house while Claire was still alive, and Anthony kept begging his little brother to try to remember. But Ron wasn't convinced. He'd seen plenty of guilty perps swear they were innocent and he could usually tell.

Yet the look on Mia's face... the way she was looking at the older brother... she bought it.

Ron had heard enough. "All right, Anthony. I think we'd better finish this down at the station. I've got to take you in."

"No, damn it. I told you I didn't do it."

"Yeah, I heard you, but I also heard your brother. Freddie caught you with the deceased. The way I see it, you killed his wife, he caught you, the two of you fought, and you knocked him down the steps. The only thing I haven't figured out is how you got rid of the body." He took a step toward Anthony, who quickly moved behind the couch. "C'mon, man, let's go in and get this done."

Mia jumped to her feet. "Ron, wait, please. Let's give him a chance. Maybe—"

"No, Mia, think what you're doing. I don't know why you even came here with him."

"I... I didn't have a choice." Mia looked from Ron to Anthony and back. Hands folded, she added, "I mean he didn't tell me where we were going. I just wanted to go home."

"So you're here against your will, yet you're defending him? Taking his side?" Ron saw the pleading in her eyes vanish.

"I'm not taking sides!" With her jaw set, she said, "I'm trying to get at the truth... which is what you should be doing."

"I am!" Ron heaved an exasperated sigh. "All right," he exclaimed. "Say what you have to say, Anthony. Let's hear it." He gave Mia his best 'are you satisfied?' look, then turned his attention to the man behind the couch—who suddenly didn't look so damned sure of himself.

"I told you," Anthony pleaded. "When I left, Claire was still alive, but she was scared. She'd seen you lose it before." Anthony shook his head at Freddie. "I shouldn't have left the house while you were in such a rage. You know how you get." Freddie looked wary. "But you were coming after me. Remember?"

Ron thought he saw a glimmer of recognition in the younger brother's eyes.

Looking back at Ron, Anthony went on. "So, I drove around for a while—not long—and knew I had to come back and try to straighten things out."

He paused so long Ron considered urging him on, but then Anthony closed his eyes and mumbled, "But I was too late."

Freddie's eyes went wide with disbelief. He seemed to be hanging on every word.

Anthony came around the sofa, and Ron's hand hovered over his gun again. But Anthony didn't make a move to leave—or to hurt anyone—he simply collapsed into the floral chair and dropped his head into his hands.

Ron relaxed his grip and looked at Mia whose eyes flitted between the two brothers.

When Anthony finally raised his head, Ron was shocked to see tears running down his face. "Freddie, I didn't mean to hurt you, but I saw Claire lying there... and all the blood... and you were still out of your mind... like when you killed Champ."

Freddie, who had been staring out the window, jerked his head back around to his brother, eyes wide, but said nothing. Ron heard no denial. Saw none in his face. *And who's Champ?*

Anthony finally turned to face the detective. "He came at me. We struggled... I was only trying to defend myself, I swear," he said glancing back at his brother. "That's when I pushed him off me, and he fell down the steps."

All eyes were on Freddie, now ashen, as the younger brother remembered. He covered his face with his hands then moaned, "*Noooo...*"

CHAPTER FORTY

Mia's head was still spinning as she recounted the events of the evening to her roommate over dinner an hour later.

"Anthony told us everything," she said. "How he'd been in such a panic that he put Claire's body in the trunk and took it to a deserted area." Mia closed her eyes then quickly opened them, not wanting to imagine the sight she was describing. "I painted the earring in the dirt, but it wasn't actually meant to be in the flower bed. It must've fallen off in the trunk when he moved her body. And then later he thought it was safe, so he went back. Said he wanted to give her a better grave. Can you imagine? But by then the police had found her body."

"But what about those text messages she sent to Anthony?... Oh... I get it now. Wow!" Morgan carried her plate to the sink. "Unreal. And by the way, I was worried sick about you, yanno. I couldn't believe it when I saw you get in the car with him. And then when you didn't answer your phone!" She rolled her eyes. "Even Simmie was worried. What were you thinking? Jesus! Oops, sorry."

"It's all right." Mia appreciated her roommate's consideration of her beliefs. "A moment of weakness, that's all. But I'm learning. I've got to stop being such a people pleaser, and trust my instincts," she said. "But no, I mean, yes it was kind of stupid, but I think I was where I needed to be. Where God wanted me to be. Besides, I'm fine. And you know, it's funny. When everything was over tonight and I was leaving the Alessi house, I saw the most beautiful rainbow in the darkening sky... and the air was so fresh and clean. It was kind of eerie, but awesome."

"And what about the jackass? You do know he's still an ass, right?"

"Yes, Morgan, and I know he's going to prison for what he's done. He didn't kill his sister-in-law, but he still broke quite a few laws trying to cover up a murder and get rid of the body." Mia shuddered. "And he lied to the police. But you know, when he said he didn't kill her, I knew he was telling the truth. I can almost feel sorry for him—"

"What?"

"No, listen. Can you imagine what he went through that night? Calling 9-1-1, knowing Claire's body was upstairs? Then rushing back to get her out of there when he realized Freddie was concussed and didn't remember anything? And wanting to get back to the hospital by the time Freddie was out of surgery so no one would suspect anything. Then all this time not knowing if his brother would remember...and I mean, if Anthony really did love Claire, what must that have been like for him?"

"Do you think he did?"

"I don't know. Maybe. As much as he knows how to love somebody. Seems to me both Alessi brothers are pretty twisted." Mia shook her head. "And did I tell you Freddie killed their dog when he was a kid? I knew he had some anger issues, but I didn't see Intermittent Explosive Disorder. Apparently Anthony has been covering up for him his whole life. And I didn't see any of it."

"Don't beat yourself up. You didn't have a complete history. Seems there were a lot of lies in that family."

"Yes," Mia said. "I'll keep them in my prayers."

"You're a good woman, Mia Reed. Little bit crazy, but good. Now, I'll clean up this mess. You've done enough for one evening," Morgan said clearing away the dishes from their very late dinner. "So, what about Ron?"

"What about him?"

"Oh, don't play coy with me. You should've seen how freaked he was when I told him you were with Anthony," Morgan said. "I think he's got a thing for you. Are you going to see him again?"

"You're crazy. You're a crazy romantic... but yes, actually. After the other police got there to take the Alessi boys off to jail, I started to leave, and he stopped me and asked if I'd have dinner with him tomorrow night."

"*Suweet!*"

Mia laughed. "Knock it off. I'm sure he probably just wants to debrief or talk about his missing sister or something."

"Don't be so sure, *little girl*," Morgan teased, knowing she and Julie were the only ones who dared call her that.

"You are a brat, and I'm going to bed."

"Ah yes, sweet dreams... about that handsome detective."

Mia laughed at her roommate's foolishness, but when at last she drifted off to sleep, her final thoughts were indeed of that handsome blue-eyed detective, Ron Bishop.

CHAPTER FORTY-ONE

The day flew by for Mia. Just one more group before she could head home. She had shot Ron a text during her lunch break asking where he wanted to meet for dinner, but she hadn't heard back before her dementia group, so she checked her phone.

Ron: How about I pick you up? 7:00 okay?

Mia: Sure. See you then.

It felt almost like a date. *But it's not a date*, she told herself. *Focus, Mia.*

When she checked the list of children from pediatrics scheduled for three o'clock, she was surprised and alarmed to see Amber Mason's name among them, but when Amber strolled into the art room, Mia was relieved to find the girl was there on an outpatient status.

Amber asked if she could do a drawing and, given approval, began sketching first then took up the colored pencils to complete it. Pulling the sketch close to her body whenever Mia passed nearby, Amber smiled slyly. Mia couldn't help wondering what her young patient was up to but respected her wishes to keep it secret.

Mia talked with each of the other children about their creations—the two youngest with their finger paintings and the three preadolescents with their collages—then finally, near the end of the hour, she approached Amber.

"May I see your drawing now?"

Amber nodded and unveiled a picture of a woman with her two daughters. Mia hadn't realized the extent of Amber's artistic skill until this moment. "This is wonderful!" she said enthusiastically. Mia recognized the people in the drawing, but to be safe, said, "Is this you with your Mom and little sister?" Another nod. "Do you know how talented you are, Amber?"

The grin that lit up the girl's face warmed Mia's heart. But she had to ask, "I don't see your father here. Can you tell me where he is?"

"He's not in the picture, because he's gone." There was no change of expression. No sign Amber was saddened by the statement. It was just a fact.

"Where did he go?" Mia asked, wondering if this was temporary... or if he was 'gone' for good. She couldn't help hoping for the latter.

"Mom said he's not coming back. She was kind of like sad at first, but she said we're gonna be fine." Amber met Mia's eyes. "And I know she's right. Thank you for helping us."

So she knew. Mia wondered who had told her—or did she just guess? It didn't really matter. What mattered was that she felt safe now.

Session ended, each of the other kids left until only Amber lingered. Mia sensed there was something more the girl needed to say.

"So, you're doing all right, huh?" Mia asked.

"Yes, ma'am." Amber got to her feet. Then she did something unexpected. She shyly approached and gave her therapist a hug. It wasn't unusual for the kids in Mia's groups to want hugs, but until now, Amber never had. Mia swallowed the lump in her throat.

Then with a slight quiver in her voice she said, "I hope you'll keep drawing, Amber. I think you could be quite a good artist someday."

Amber's whole face smiled when she said, "I will. I want to do art and help people like you do someday."

Mia batted her eyes to keep the tears from leaking out until the girl was gone, then, alone in the art room, she grabbed a tissue and let them fall freely.

"Hey girl, oh my gosh, what's wrong?" Morgan asked rushing to her side.

Mia hadn't heard her roommate come in and struggled to choke out her response. "I'm okay."

"Yeah right, I can tell." Morgan got a cup of water from the sink in the back of the room and grabbed the tissue box, giving Mia a chance to compose herself. "All right, now. Talk to me. What happened? Don't tell me Mr. Detective canceled on you."

"No. No, don't be silly... and why would that upset me anyway?" Mia managed between sniffs, but she didn't miss Morgan's raised eyebrows. After giving her nose a good blow, she tried to explain. "These were really happy tears. I mean, one of my patients—you remember Amber?—well, before she left she gave me the best possible compliment. And, it was so touching I teared up, that's all, and... well, and then once I started to cry, I couldn't stop." Mia giggled nervously. "Once I opened the floodgates, yanno?"

"All right, yeah, probably because of all you've been through lately. But that's over now." Morgan gave Mia a final hug then held her at arm's length. "And you're sure you're okay now?"

Mia nodded.

"All righty then. You'd better finish up here and get going. You've gotta get ready for your hot date tonight."

"It's not a date!" Mia called to her retreating roommate.

Two hours later, as she stood staring into her closet unable to decide what to wear, she repeated the thought, *It's not a date.* So what was the big deal? *Just pick something.* Still as she pictured those blue eyes, she couldn't help but compare them to Anthony's brown eyes, so full of deceit.

Mia knew Ron's eyes could be trusted, and she realized she was anxious to see them again. They were true blue.

CHAPTER FORTY-TWO

Settling on the loose-fitting gold tunic and black slacks, Mia searched her meager jewelry box for the right earrings. When her eyes landed on the small gold and black hoops, she decided they were perfect.

After a quick assessment in the mirror, she knew she was ready. Or was she overdressed? *Stop it!* 6:45. With fifteen minutes to wait—unless he was a jerk like Anthony and kept her waiting longer—Mia meandered into her solarium. She picked up her most recent painting, the landscape, and carried it into the living room.

She jumped at the knock on the door... 6:48. When she answered it, she was relieved to see she hadn't overdressed. Ron Bishop was looking quite debonair in his chinos, blazer, and light blue dress shirt.

"Sorry I'm early," he said.

"That's okay, come in. I just have to grab my bag." Mia dashed into the bedroom to get her clutch, leaving Ron alone in the living room. When she returned, she found him staring at the painting she'd left on the coffee table. "What do you think?"

"What?"

"I said, what do you think? Do you like it?"

"Oh... yes. Definitely. Your paintings are beautiful," he said looking back at the picture. Mia waited, but he didn't move.

"Is something wrong?"

"What? Oh, no. It's just that there's something so familiar about this scene. It reminds me of someplace, but I can't quite put my finger on it." He finally took his eyes off the painting when Simeon decided to make one of his rare appearances and rubbed up against Ron's leg.

"Oh, I'm sorry. Simmie stop! He'll shed all over you," Mia said scooping him up in her arms. "He usually makes himself scarce when he sees a stranger."

"Don't worry about it." Ron laughed as he reached over and stroked the beautiful gray fur. "I like cats, and he's a beauty." Ron looked at Mia's painting then back at Mia and smiled. "There seems to be a lot that's beautiful here. And I'm not just talking about your cat or your painting," he said.

Mia hadn't expected that, and searched frantically for a reply. A simple "Thank you" colored her cheeks. There was a sudden awkwardness in the room and Mia guessed Ron had surprised himself as well. "Okay, Simmie, off with you," she said dropping him into her spot on the beast. "You can keep my seat warm for me."

Purse in hand, she turned back to face Ron.

"So, um, do you like Mexican food?" he asked.

"Love it!"

"Great... I mean, are you sure? We can do Italian or seafood or whatever you'd like."

"I love Mexican," Mia said thinking how different Ron was from Anthony—how considerate.

"Okay, good," Ron said. "I thought maybe we could go to Emiliano's. It's not far from here."

Located right on Carson Street, it didn't take long to get there, and Mia was surprised by the effortlessness with which they chatted on the way. The awkwardness she'd felt at the apartment completely evaporated with easy conversation over shared nachos, and Mia found her eyes continually meeting his. She feared she was becoming completely mesmerized and was saved only by the arrival of their entrees.

Mia had ordered the Cancun Chimichanga and was not disappointed. Ron was enjoying his Carnitas and they each tried the other's dish in a fashion that reminded Mia of the way her parents so often did. She was surprised at how comfortable she was with this man she'd known for such a short time.

"That was great," Ron said putting his fork down on an empty plate. "Maybe next time we can share the Parrillada Grill Dinner for two."

Next time? Mia watched him shake his head and blink, realizing what he was suggesting.

"I mean... all right, that was kind of presumptuous of me," he said, and Mia could have sworn it was his cheeks showing a bit of a blush this time, and she found it enchanting. "But, well, I hope there will be a next time." He looked at her expectantly.

"I think I'd like to try the Parrillada Grill Dinner for two."

Mia liked the way his face relaxed with a slow sexy smile that went from his lips to his eyes.

"Did you want coffee?" he asked.

"How about we go back to my place and I can make some good coffee... or you could try one of my wonderful teas?"

"I'll stick with coffee, thanks."

A little later, lingering over their hot beverages, with neither seeming anxious to have the evening end, they did eventually talk about Ron's missing twin, and when they did, Ron got a faraway look in his eyes.

"What is it?" she asked

"Do you mind if I take another look at that painting?"

Mia got it for him and watched him diving into it.

"What is it?" she asked again. "Do you recognize something?" Mia could no longer doubt the power of her paintings, the special ones.

Ron pulled his eyes from the landscape and looking up said, "Yes, I think I know this place. It looks like where Mom and Dad took us when we were kids." He shook his head from side to side. "If I could just remember where it was."

"Why don't you take it with you? Maybe it will come to you." Mia felt the power of the painting... the power of the Holy Spirit's gift.

It was about that time when Morgan came in from having dinner with some of the other nurses at the hospital. After greeting the detective and her roommate, she discreetly made herself scarce saying she had some reading to do.

Once Morgan's bedroom door closed, Ron said, "I'd better be going. We both have work tomorrow."

He got to his feet, and Mia sprang to hers as well, and the two walked to the door.

Ron turned to Mia, gently put his hands on her arms. "May I kiss you goodnight?"

Warmed by the fact he had asked, she simply nodded and lifted her face when Ron brought his lips to meet hers.

Mia felt something she hadn't ever felt before. Not the simple passion she'd experienced with others. Ron's soft lips, the tenderness of his kiss, went deeper—to a place she'd never been—but somewhere she knew she would return to again and again.

WHISPERED WARNINGS

SNEAK PREVIEW

It was a stroke—not of luck, but of a brain blockage—that was about to change Mia Reed's life and take her away from Pittsburgh and everything familiar and comfortable in her new life as an art therapist.

Stunned, she clutched her phone, barely noticing when Simeon jumped in her lap to comfort her. She stared out the window, absently stroking the cat's silver-gray fur with her free hand.

"I'd better get going before..." Morgan took one look at her roommate and put on the brakes before reaching the door. "What's wrong?"

"My mom called. It... it's my grandpa." Mia lowered her head, letting her light brown hair hide the tears. "He... he had a stroke."

"Oh Mia, I'm so sorry. What can I do? Is he..." Morgan didn't finish her sentence, but Mia knew what she was asking.

"No. No, Grandma was there when it happened and called 9-1-1. He's in the emergency room, and she's there with him. They're all at the hospital..." The words trailed off as Mia stared out the window. "I should be there."

Mia crumpled on the couch, and her roommate quickly sat next to her and took her hand. "Can I get you some water or something? Maybe tea?" Mia appreciated that, even though she was only four years younger than her roommate, Morgan had a tendency to look after her. Mia assumed it was because she looked much younger than her twenty-three years, and perhaps, as she'd often been told, because she was somewhat naïve.

"No, no, I'm okay. I mean, I don't need anything. But..." When the tears Mia had been holding back started rushing down her cheeks, Morgan ran for the tissues. "Aren't you going to be late?" Mia managed to ask between sobs.

"Don't be silly. Lunch with the girls on our floor is no big deal," Morgan said pulling out her phone and texting a quick message. "I know I'm the comic relief, but they can manage one lunch without me."

Mia attempted to smile, but there was no sign of her usual dimple as she gave it up and blew her nose. "I want to go home," she said still stroking Simeon who, determined to help, nuzzled under her chin.

"Of course you do, and you won't have any trouble getting time off."

"No, Morgan. I mean yes, I need to get some time off right away, but I need more than that. I don't want to be this far away from my family every time something happens." Mia stared out the window of their small southside apartment that she and Morgan had shared for the last few years. She had created a comfortable life here, as comfortable as the oversized brown chair they called the big brown beast... the only thing holding her up at the moment. But there was another place calling her away. Calling her home. "I should be there when they need me."

"I get that, and I know it must feel that way now, but you couldn't have done anything if you'd been there. I'm sure everything's going to be okay."

"You don't understand, Morgan. This isn't the first time I've thought about it. I know it may sound crazy—I'm not a child—but I miss my family. I miss being near them and seeing them whenever I want." Mia looked up at her roommate. "I don't want to desert you and leave you stuck with no one to share expenses, but I've been considering it for a while, and I think I want to move somewhere closer to my hometown. Closer to my family."

Morgan's face lost all its usual animation. With her eyes cast down, she nodded. "I can't say I'm shocked," she said. "I know how you feel about your family, and honestly, if I had a family like yours, I guess I'd want to spend more time with them too." Morgan patted Mia's hand. "Don't worry. With my winning personality, I'll find another roommate in no time. But where will you live, and where will you work? And what about Ron?"

Yeah, what about Ron? Mia's relationship with Detective Ronald Bishop was still new and she wondered if it could survive the distance. "I know. I've got a lot to figure out," she said, getting up slowly and moving toward her bedroom, "but right now I've got to make a few phone calls and pack. I want to get to Madison by early evening."

***

The trip home began smoothly on that sunny, summer afternoon, but two hours into the drive Mia hit a gray wall of torrential rain. Bolts of lightning cut through the purple sky ahead, joined almost immediately by thunder like a drummer gone mad. She wasn't shocked by the downpour since this August had been filled with hot humid days, many of which turned into angry afternoon storms followed by calm and beautiful rainbows. *But this is ridiculous!* With the windshield wipers working frantically to give her a tiny bit of visibility, Mia squinted to keep the taillights of the car in front of her within sight while she searched for another rest area to pull off the turnpike. She didn't see anywhere to exit the highspeed highway until she was passing the off-ramps and too late to make the turn.

Luckily, before long she'd driven through the storm and could lower her shoulders from her ears. Mia turned off the windshield wipers, gave thanks for the bright sunshine, and searched the sky for one of those rainbows.

But the lovely respite was not to last. Long before she reached her exit, Mia could see the next storm front, and passing through this curtain of rain was like rushing headlong from daylight into a dangerous dungeon of darkness.

Mia leaned forward. She turned the radio way down so she could see better. Fingers clenched in a death grip on the steering wheel, her nerves were raw. Then the cell phone shrieked. Mia jumped at the sound. She fumbled to grab the device and read the screen: *Tornado warning!* Having passed the last rest-stop on this part of the turnpike, there was no escape... nowhere to go to get out of the storm. Beyond panic, she thought, *Why did I say no?*

When she'd called Ron to tell him what was going on, he had offered to drive her home, but Mia thought that was ridiculous. Since starting at Seton Hill University, she had made the drive from Pittsburgh to her hometown enough times to almost do it in her sleep. And though he said it would be a good excuse to spend more time with her, Mia was sure the man she was falling in love with was actually worried about her driving while upset over her grandfather.

"I am not a child," she had argued. *"And I'm totally capable of keeping my emotions under control while I drive."* It was their first disagreement—if you could even call it that—since Mia and Detective Ronald Bishop had started seeing each other. Ever since that terrifying night at the Alessi house when she'd thought a suspected murderer might end her life, she and Ron had been spending as much time together as their schedules allowed, and as soon as they said their goodbyes, Mia would look forward to the next time she'd see him.

But now she had to find a way to tell him she was leaving Pittsburgh permanently. *Am I crazy?*

Another crack of thunder called her attention back to the task before her—getting to Madison, Pennsylvania, and not Oz. *God, please keep me safe.* And from within she heard the familiar *"Trust in the Lord."*

Though the storm didn't let up until Mia was nearly home, she saw no sign of a tornado—the only whirlwind was in her mind which calmed when she reached Madison General and the arms of her family.

She soon learned Grandpa Reed would probably have a long recovery, but with time and therapy, he should fully regain the use of his left side. And Mia knew somehow everything else would be okay too. She had many decisions to make—questions for which she must find answers—but the important thing right now was being with family. As for the rest, she decided, like Scarlett O'Hara, *I'll think about that tomorrow.*

And Mia knew, somehow, she must find a way for her tomorrows to include Ron Bishop.

ABOUT THE AUTHOR

Gloria Bostic is a retired special education teacher from York, Pennsylvania. As a Masters level clinical psychologist, she also worked with women and children to help them overcome abuse. She lives in Dover, PA, with her husband, Lee, and enjoys spending time with her three sons and grandchildren.

Also by Gloria Bostic...

Deception Bridge (Book 1)

Valerie Reed is plagued by migraines, insomnia, and a growing anxiety that her happily-ever-after is about to come crumbling down. Tormented by the fear of losing her husband of nearly thirty years, she hangs onto the one thing she knows she can count on – her friendship with the women in her bridge group. They provide a safe-haven with warmth, laughter, and trust... until that trust is broken.

As Val searches for a way to save her marriage and learn to trust again, her life and her bridge group go through unanticipated transformations. Their lives will never be the same, and Val wonders if the power of prayer will be enough to save them all.

Broken Contracts (Book 2)

Through faith and forgiveness Valerie and Andy Reed's marriage has survived and grown stronger in spite of Andy's brief affair five years ago. However, the consequences of his tryst with Susan Walters, a former member of Val's bridge group, may now turn their world upside-down once again.

As Susan's marriage falls apart, all she wants is to be a good mother to the child she had always longed for... yet her life is becoming unmanageable as she continually succumbs to the need for her next drink.

When Valerie, Bonnie, Sarah, and Kathy gather around the bridge table, they share more than the game. Only time will tell what's in the cards.

Premonition Bridge (Book 3)

A threat... A former client warns that her husband is wildly angry that she left him and blames her therapist, Sarah Reed, for ruining his life. He vows to get even.

A disappearance... A member of the Reed family mysteriously disappears without a trace. The only clues to the victim's whereabouts may come from mystifying messages in drawings and dreams.

A reuniting... Family members separated, relationships lost, friendships dissolved... Will prayer and forgiveness be enough for the bridge club ladies to find resolution from the chaos that has invaded their lives?

Out of the Storm

Greta Friedman travels from victim to victory in this story of a young woman's search for the life she's been denied. A childhood filled with loss and abuse leaves her desperate to find love and normalcy, but as a young adult Greta is frustrated by unanswered prayers and a pattern of relationships that end badly... until she meets someone special. When Gabe Engel mysteriously comes into her life, Greta begins the journey that will give her the strength to escape impending danger and finally make her dreams a reality.

The Greatest Aunt

It's a scary time for Flora when she learns her parents must go away. She will have to go live with her great-aunt, but can't understand why they call her great. Flora happily discovers why and agrees!